KHAOS ENGINE

D R LINTON

Britain's Next
BESTSELLER

First published in 2019 by:
Britain's Next Bestseller
An imprint of Live It Ventures LTD

www.bnbsbooks.co.uk

All enquiries should be addressed to Britain's Next Bestseller
126 Kirkleatham Lane,
Redcar. Cleveland.
Ts10 5DD
@BNBSbooks

ISBN 978-190695-447-5
Cover designed by Miacello

Special thanks to:
Donna Linton
Faye Daly
Naomi Linton

PREFACE

There is a theory which states that a small change at one place in a nonlinear system can result in large differences to a later state, and that nature most often works in patterns, which are caused by the sum of many tiny pulses.

Simply summarised, one single source can affect multiple elements.

Never underestimate the inevitability of unpredictability...

PART 1

PART 1

A LONDON NIGHTCLUB KICKS OUT FOR THE NIGHT

Prologue

The time is 3:17am and Christopher is being followed, but the footsteps aren't audible.

Even at this hour, these East End streets are a quiet and non-incidental affair nowadays, and Chris, after a skinful (and, as it's Friday, a nose full) has recently taken to exploring new short cuts over to the cheaper and less publicised taxi rank across town. His destination is his Hackney 1 bed. Tonight, his route of choice is Bennett Street, down the side of the old cracker factory. Chris is no stranger to the sensation of being followed, and standing at a strapping 6'4" and weighing in at 16.5 stone, he's no slouch when a tear up is on the cards. Tonight though, for some reason, Chris doesn't turn immediately, fists flying when he hears a low and constant exhaling of breath followed by a muffled gargled growl; a strange sickly sweet aroma fills the cool, black air.

Maybe Chris is mistaken and just para from the Charlie, he walks a few more yards.

Sigh… growl.

The sickly-sweet smell hit's the back of Chris' throat, making him gag. Unease turns to fear, and a stumbling swagger is replaced by a brisk jog. A separate voice bursts the frigid night air like a cannonball.

"ADHERENCE IS OBLIGATORY!"

The sound resonates through Chris' body like an electric shock. Someone grabs him by the tops of his arms, Chris knows it's on; he has been grabbed like that before, and it didn't end well for his assailant. He shrugs, planning to use his formidable core strength to switch the situation in his favour. Nothing. His captor is stronger than he is, and, for the first time in his adult life, Chris is being overpowered, dominated. He grits his teeth and cries out as he convulses, desperately expending the last of his strength.

No good.

Chris submits and waits for the inevitable blunt impact to the back of the head or the invasion of cold steel in his side. He shuts his eyes tight, flashes of his first unaided bike ride, first shag, first line of coke. But wait… no impact, no cold steel.

Sigh… growl… hiss!

Chris is scared but confusion now circles his mind like a whirlwind. That voice, that separate voice in a shrill knowing tone, rattles Chris bones and fills the night once again.

"ADHERENCE IS OBLIGATORY!"

Those words, although familiar, don't make any sense, as if he is staring at a few random jigsaw pieces from a picture he knows very well. Suddenly, an abrupt and blunt pain shudders down the centre of Chris' chest. The pain is so intense that his eyes blur for a second. But it's not a blade. Chris squeals out in agony.

A loud *snap* cuts the air.
Please be a passer-by…

PART 2

ANDREW DAX – INTRODUCTION TO THE BORING NEUROTIC

My name is Andrew and I've been told that I think too deeply about things.

Now exactly what that means or how I should respond to such analysis is open to subjective interpretation. The fact that I am the lead data analyst for the 2nd largest company on the planet isn't impressive, and to go into detail on the intricacies of my role would be to grab you by the foot and drag you down into the blank vortex of boredom that my life has become.

I get this very odd but deeply unsettling feeling when I am just about to fall asleep. Late at night, as I drift towards REM, I'm filled with the sudden notion that it isn't sleep I am drifting into but something altogether more permanent. A feeling that if I don't rouse myself immediately that the cold arms of death will indeed embrace me too tightly for me to provide adequate resistance. I connect this feeling with the City of London. Somehow it feels like London itself is stuck on this precipice. Like the capital is paused in that dreadful moment, unable to rouse itself.

Me? Andrew Dax? Thinking too deeply about things? Nonsense!

Seriously though, there may be a kernel of truth in the diagnosis. You see, for the last six months or so, I've been suffering from anxiety attacks, utterly new and completely random.

These episodes have gradually increased in intensity by the week.

I finally decided that I needed help, when 3 weeks ago, I fled my place of employment in a thinly veiled state of panic.

This attack struck in the middle of the day, so I had to blame my impromptu disappearance on a sudden bout of sickness and diarrhoea. How attractive.

Very close friends and family have reacted with genuine surprise at this sudden affliction. I'm not really sure why this is.

I guess part of this might be due

to my bad habit of randomly shutting down and letting sarcasm slip into my dialogue, I frequently do this when I'm uncomfortable or placed on the spot. You see, I hate confrontation, and ever since my formative years I've used this method to either get me out of tight squeezes, or gain me credibility. People I meet often get the patently wrong impression that I'm unflappable.

Anyway, the whys and the wherefores are of no consequence. It is a real problem that I have developed, and it's now genuinely starting to infringe on my day to day life, so it needs sorting.

So this is part of my therapy...

What is, you ask?

This, what I am writing, right now.

Let me explain myself. Since my little freak out, I've started seeing a counsellor. This counsellor has suggested that I start a blog of life (pretentious, moi?). This particular blog will never be uploaded, or shared with anyone. It sounds pointless, doesn't it, keeping a diary, written in the style of a shared blog, but never actually publishing it? Well, yes, it does feel strange, but apparently writing, and particularly writing in this way is very therapeutic, plus it's a method of writing that is already familiar to me.

So, I guess it's worth a try, and hey, it isn't costing me anything. So here goes…

PART 3

ANDREW DAX (BLOG ENTRY)

I am Andrew Dax, Corporate Cog.

Ezekiel Cleaver is my boss. Not my direct boss but my *boss* boss if you follow. I've opted to begin this little ritual by rambling on about the company that employs me for a while. As I have already confirmed, my particular job within this company is way too bland and uninspiring to even attempt to explain. It's the business itself which is important, and, dare I say, rather interesting.

I believe this starting point is as good as any.

The reason why I earlier alluded to England's capital city is because that is where I reside and work.

Twenty-three years ago, London Metropolitan Police was in complete disarray, not just from a fiscal standpoint, but also from a repetitional angle.

Crime was up to crisis level and there simply weren't enough resources to contain it. The stink of fear on the streets, shopping centres and tube stations was so palpable you could almost reach out and grasp it. Move quickly and quietly, avoiding eye contact at all costs and try to stick to populated areas. These were the basics of city survival at the time. Trends and types of violent crime had taken an almost artistic twist in terms of severity and brutality, as if the most damaged minds had realised that this was their time, their holiday, and my word were they going to enjoy it! Making sure they collected plenty of treasured memories for years to come.

The disorder wasn't by any means unique to the capital; but London was- by volume alone- the most unsafe place to be. There were attempts to curb this national epidemic mind, the boldest being the U-turn on the death penalty bill. Pre-meditating murderers, repeating violent criminals along with the vilest sexual deviants, could all now legally be destroyed. "Good!" I hear you cry, however this only functioned as a sticking plaster and didn't actually serve as a cure.

The funding cuts imposed by the then government at the time had been so severe that instead of bringing promised equilibrium, they had completely backfired leading to mass redundancies and enforced "restructuring". Almost every public service provider countrywide was running on less than skeleton staff, not least London Met.

The truth was a simple one: London, and by extension, England was on its knees and needed saving. Enter Ezekiel Cleaver.

Cleaver began his journey to international heroism as a Physicist working for the British Space Programme as was. His specialisms were quantum chemistry, surfaces, and solid state physics.

At this stage I feel I should admit that I am very aware of the danger of getting bogged down in rambling details, I will try and avoid this.

Approximately 35 years ago, (I know this via media and not because I was there) Cleaver was heavily in involved with a project called Grosvenor. This involved the exploration of Venus. At that time a lot had already been learned of the secrets that Mars had to share, and contrary to the romanticism of the arts, the findings were something of an anti-climax. The US were not remotely interested in the project at this stage, and refused to commit financially, while a new look and ambitious British Space programme forged ahead unabashed. The fact that project Grosvenor was allowed to rumble on with minimal interest or scrutiny from both media and the rest the world is an important one.

For some reason, I am reminded of an unsettling news story from around five or six years ago. Just off the Gulf of Mexico a 50 metre diameter sinkhole suddenly introduced itself and took 13 locals with it. I remember thinking to myself, "Wow, God's getting kind of creative with his natural disasters!"

But I digress. Grosvenor itself came and went without too much incident, a few Astral Engineers (Astronauts with spanners) went up tinkered around, drilled a few really deep holes, and came down again, in one piece, happy days. One of those Astral Engineers went by the name of Richard Lloyd.

There is a living organism which resides approximately 22 meters under the surface of Venus; its molecular structure is so unstable that once out of its natural habitat it has to be kept at a very exact temperature, in a precisely controlled atmosphere. Failing to do this would cause anyone within a 100 yard radius more than a little skin and bone problem. To the human eye it is oil slick black in colour and texture and has no particular shape; as a mass it is constantly moving. The fact that it is constantly changing shape and size whilst suspended, along with the knowledge that it proves there is life on Venus is unarguably interesting.

However it's interesting in the same way that finding out that all Best Before dates on packets of crisps manufactured in the UK fall on a Saturday.

The real reason I am telling you about this is that a portion of this element was taken during project Grosvenor and brought to the BSP's main lab and eventually labelled Niroplaxia Gamonite.

After months of testing and retesting, it was found that this organism if correctly harnessed could serve as a perpetual of source electrical energy.

Now it would be insulting to say this was momentous, it would be an understatement to call it world changing, the best way that I can think of (or maybe it was a newspaper headline) to describe what happened back then is to say that is was one of the most important discoveries in the history of mankind.

Its discoverer was named Richard Lloyd, its developer? Ezekiel Cleaver.

Niroplaxia Gamonite is more commonly known as the Lloyd-Cleaver Element. Cleaver legally owns the LC Element. The way one man came to own one of the most important discoveries in the history of mankind has something to do with a man named Vincent Gwiazda.

Vincent Gwiazda is dead.

1

"Three fatalities! Talk to me Felix! 17 years of nothing and then three fatalities?? How? Talk to me Felix, you're my Robot man!"

Ezekiel Cleaver boomed, his face contorted in a mixture of rage and confusion. The "Robot Man" was Felix Baxter, mechanical and hydraulics whizz kid and Head of Robotics at Computer Cop Corp. The only thing more impressive than Cleaver's unbelievable mental capacity was his almost preternatural gift of unearthing and surrounding himself with similar freaks of nature. Computer Cop Corp or CCC was one of several companies that reside under the Cleaver Corp umbrella. It was founded 21 years ago by Ezekiel Cleaver along with silent partner and chief benefactor Vincent Gwiazda.

The fatalities that Cleaver spoke of were a result of two separate and very high profile drone malfunctions. Computerized Law Enforcement Drones known commonly as "CLEDS" or "Com Cops" had been patrolling the streets of Central and East London for the past 17 years. The units were originally packaged as Police Support Drones, and introduced as an enhancement to the regular manned force. They now boasted a 40% share of all police activity. So successful were these state of the art pieces of engineering, that national rollout was predicted to take just 5 years.

Cleaver dropped back down to his chair, he wasn't a small man, but today he cut a tiny figure, shrunk behind his huge desk, in the corner of his vast, all white furnished, semi-circular office. Baxter couldn't recall ever seeing his boss, everybody's boss like this. He usually filled the room, metaphorically of course; such was the man's quiet yet steely demeanor. Baxter met Cleaver in Spain at a seminar, longer ago than he cared to remember. Over the years he had become one of the mogul's very few "close men".

"I… I've been working on both drones since the start of the week, testing and retesting, trying to determine whether it was a data or a mechanical problem," mumbled Baxter. "Problem?"croaked Cleaver, "my god man a guy in his late 20's…"

"Yes, but we…"

"Then a young mother along with her 5 year old daughter in broad bloody day light!"

"Yes, but Ezekiel?"

"DR CLEAVER! Today my name is Dr Cleaver," hissed the incensed CEO.

"Dr Cleaver," Baxter whispered. "What happened with units 8 and 14 was completely unprecedented, nothing like this has ever come close to happening, never even a near-miss to speak of. CLEDs just aren't programmed in that way. The programme notes and history for both units show no obvious discrepancies. Although mechanical defects wouldn't result in these actions… no all signs point towards deliberate command tampering, but how?" Baxter was now thinking aloud to himself, in the way that academics often do when locked in analytical musing. Cleaver slammed his palm down on his desk to refocus Baxter and leaned forward, lowering his voice.

"Felix listen to me very carefully, we have two meetings in the next 3 months, one with Greater Manchester and one with West Midlands. Each of these meetings could conclude with two separate purchase orders for 20 Drones. Over the last 5 days two of these Drones have brutally killed 3 innocent members of the public, apparently without command or warning. What is wrong with this picture?"

"I...I"

Cleaver cut him short.

"Let me explain to you what happens next: I give you 1 week to at least give me the foundation work of a theory into how this came about and, believe me, your job absolutely depends on it".

Cleaver had only threatened Felix Baxter's job one other time in their lengthy working relationship. Cleaver continued, "in the meantime I will speak to PR and see if there is anything...ANYTHING we can do to stop the rot from a media point of view. I take it all Drones are in lock up?"

"Yes, Dr Cleaver."

CLEAVER CORP

Cleaver Corp was a large multinational conglomerate, whose main offering consisted of research and development in the fields of molecular science, energy transformation, sustainable energy and robotics. Computer Cop Corp was mainly a robotics branch of the organisation based at the Sanhedrin building in Stratford, East London. It was developed off the back of Cleaver Corp's successful bid to take full control of a newly privatised Metropolitan Police Force. The Sanhedrin replaced New Scotland Yard as London's Police Headquarters, with all remaining constabularies around London taking on Cleaver Corp's branding.

Dr Ezekiel Benjamin Cleaver is a celebrated Physicist and founder and CEO of Cleaver Corp.

There was a common misconception surrounding the story of Ezekiel Cleaver and Richard Lloyd, most would have been led to believe that the reason Cleaver gained sole ownership of the LC Element was because of Richard Lloyd's mysterious disappearance. However this is incorrect, as Lloyd actually signed over his ownership rights wholly to Cleaver a full 3 months before his disappearance.

This was, for all intents and purposes, completely legal and above board. There were four men present that day, both Lloyd, and Cleaver made the agreement under the watchful eye of main benefactor Vincent Gwiazda and acting as an official witness was the then Head of Engineering William Foxworthy. The men figured that as Foxworthy wasn't a money man, he would be the closest thing to a neutral party.

William Foxworthy was one of the original Space Programme "Deserters", he walked away from BSP to join Cleaver in his fledgling venture "Cleaver Corp". At that time Cleaver Corp's main source of revenue was the Total Security Drone or TSD. These were sold to private security companies worldwide, and were a great success. Foxworthy was largely responsible for the design and functionality of what would eventually become the CLED.

LLOYD AND CLEAVER had been firm friends long before Project Grosvenor; in fact it was Lloyd himself that approached the board suggesting they give the young and relatively inexperienced Scientist a "crack" at analysing the strange living substance. The programme lab's more experienced heads had completed their tests, and decided that this "gift" from Venus wasn't of much use to this particular spinning rock that we call home, due to its unstable nature.

Richard Lloyd was named Chief Astral Engineer for Project Grosvenor, having been a gifted mechanical fitter at base. He was a vibrant and well humoured character with an eternally positive outlook on life. It was this jovial swagger contrasted with his exceptional mechanical ability which first intrigued a young, shy Cleaver.

Whether it was the fact that Lloyd was 7 years the scientist's senior, or that Cleaver was the only other black employee based at BSP's head office, we may never know, but Lloyd took Cleaver under his wing and felt somehow responsible for him. Cleaver was quiet, pensive and non-confrontational; nonetheless Lloyd saw in his eyes a depth of thought that was disarming. Some of their early conversations had left Richard Lloyd reeling at the almost fathomless stream of social, moral and scientific commentary flowing forth from the young scientist.

There was also an almost otherworldly determination and commitment that underpinned all of Cleaver's endeavours. Cleaver would go off on one of his intensely captivating monologues (monologue is used here because although these exchanges were two way conversations, there was absolutely no chance that Lloyd could follow Cleaver intellectually after a certain point.), Lloyd would think to himself, "if this is the future of "Black Britain" then the leadership of this country is going to look very different in the coming decades."

24 years ago almost to the date, Richard Lloyd "dematerialized". The reason why this description is commonly used in place of "disappeared" is because of the circumstances. On that fateful night, Lloyd's partner had returned home from her late shift at the local hospital, to find the house empty. However the doors were all locked from the inside, the TV was on, there was a half tumbler of whiskey on the coffee table beside a still–smouldering cigar - Lloyd was a keen Cuban cigar and single malt enthusiast – although this was a moderately enjoyed pastime. These facts are just a brief summary of the bizarre list of contrary evidences that surround this tale. His car was still on the drive, and there was no sign of forced entry or struggle. Richard Lloyd literally vanished where he sat that night and was never seen or heard from again. The story went on to become an established part of British folk law.

PART 4

ANDREW DAX (BLOG ENTRY)

Rodger is a tool.

Sorry, let me explain myself, Rodger is one of the team leaders that I manage. Rodger also wants my job and because he's older than I am, in his world that means he's more entitled to my job than me. He is rude, arrogant and finally, as previously mentioned, a massive tool.

Rodger Brown is just one of the reasons that my walk through the rats' maze of security scanners that line the entrance to the Sanhedrin has been getting slower by the week. From the outside my job seems incredibly boring, and in recent months it has started to feel that way from the inside too. I'm good at my job. This is because I'm an analytical thinker, I have a photographic memory and my attention to detail is second to none. I am not good at my job because I'm a "natural" or some sort of "whizz Kid" or even because I am feeding a lifelong passion for computers.

The Sanhedrin is the building in which I ply my increasingly soul destroying trade. Recently, my walk up towards it every morning, as lower Stratford Street opens up to reveal the colossal structure, a quiet apprehension breezes over me. I guess the most obvious conviction would be to blame this on my freak out some weeks back, you know, maybe a kind of avoidance trigger. That apprehension has gradually been superseded by mild anxiety. So to summarize, building and company =unexplained unease, job itself = mind pulping boredom.

I have to admit, putting my personal feelings regarding my job within this increasingly foreboding building aside for a minute, the Sanhedrin itself is nothing short of a masterpiece of modern architecture. All dark marble, slick shiny fibreglass and brushed steel. As a complex it straddles both Stratford and Hackney. Its grandiose name, I've been told, is something to do with Jewish Law, but don't quote me on that. I personally don't see what was wrong with Scotland Yard, you know maybe calling it "New, New Scotland Yard. Maybe not.

There is a palpable nervous energy in the

air this morning, people are moving quicker and quieter, some are avoiding eye contact, others are mumbling to each other, their mouths hidden under their morning paper. The atmos has been like this all week — today is Thursday if you're remotely interested. If I were to hazard a guess as to why this has been the case since Monday morning, I would say it's because over the weekend prior, 3 people had been killed by a couple of Cleaver-Bots that had gone all "EXTERMINATE" on us. Now please don't think I am deliberately attempting to belittle or make light of the situation, I often use humour as a defence mechanism. I personally don't trust the things at all and always give them an extra wide berth when I'm out and about. The fact that I work for the company that make them, is just a twist of horrible irony.

The official name for these machines is Computerized Law Enforcement Drones but most call them Com Cops or CLEDs. The term "law enforcement" is key here, because I am old and ugly enough to remember London without CLEDs, and I am sure the old Met with all its flaws was mainly about "Protect and Serve". However, we seem to be moving towards being a City where law is "enforced" in its purest sense, extracting all emotion, sentiment and duty of care, law imposition, if you will. To me, the

CLEDs absolutely embody the beginning of this. It reminds me of something I overheard Cleaver say to a French diplomat after a round table a year or so ago — as one the head geeks I often get invited to these — lucky me! I didn't catch it all but the terms "my vision" and "Absolute Law Enforcement" pulsated frequently. Those kinds of terms would fill the more right leaning ear-wiggers with a sense of safety and anticipation. Nonetheless, for me it was as if an icy glass of water had been poured down the centre of my back. I don't trust CLEDs, I never have, and what happened over the weekend has only served to compound my deepest fears.

I am holding an emergency meeting this morning with my team, regarding some irregular data readings I have been picking up over the last couple of days. I know what you're thinking - but the data that we pick up in my particular team comes from the Portentis Engine via the computer room. Thus, is no way connected to the CLED killings.

Put simply we pick up readings, kicked out by the engine which is situated in the "Sub Cellar" around 20 metres below the ground floor. The raw readings are intermittent waves of compressing and decompressing chemical reactions which we call "pulses". The pulses travel up the building where they are processed via the computer room situated on the second to top floor. We pick it up at stage three;

we reside in an office around midway up. Why it was decided that the information takes such a strangled route, God only knows.

There had been a sense of apprehension floating in the air that actually pre-dates the "weekend everything changed". This is because of the Big Pulse 2 weeks ago.

The sonar style pulses that the engine puts out are usually quite discrete, often inaudible. Typically they are only registered as a small, strange popping in the ears, and even then you would only start to feel them if you venture below the ground floor. We geeks have no reason to do this with any regularity, that's Mole country. That being said, over the last 6 weeks or so there had been one strong-ish pulse a day, one that everyone bar maybe the top 4 floors, would feel. This led up to the Big Pulse. It was around a fortnight ago, a Tuesday if I recall correctly, about 3ish. It actually took a few people off their feet, brought paintings down, stopped lifts and even smashed a window over in PR (shame, that). It was more than a little worrying. The tremor was felt around the surrounding areas, within about a mile radius. This obviously led to unwanted media interest.

Mark Barker, the facilities manager sent

an "all staff" memo around stating the pulses where being "looked into" and urging us not to "be alarmed". Easier said than done Barker, you pillock!

Man, I'm irritable today!

2

Dax: Hello

Baxter: *I need to speak Andrew Dax, he oversees this department, does he not?*

Dax: *Who's calling?*

Baxter: *I need to speak to Andrew Dax, it's urgent, please!*

Dax: *Ok, ok, this is he. Now is there any chance I can ask who this is?*

Baxter: *Sorry Andy. Hi, it's Felix, Felix Baxter down in robotics?*

Dax: *Oh yeah, ok, hi Felix, what can I do for you mate? You sound a little stressed, you're not being cornered by Unit 22 as we speak are you?*

Baxter: *Yeah good one, listen I need a word with you urgently.*

Dax: *Ok, go on.*

Baxter: *No, it has to be face to face and it has to be today, have you got any gaps?*

Dax: *Ok easy, well this morning's out, got an impromptu meeting with the guys. Erm lets see... I am free 2 through to 3.*

Baxter: *Brilliant, I will see you at 2 sharp.*

Dax: *Ok man, see you then*

Baxter: *Oh, and don't come down to me, I'll come up to you.*

Dax: *Hey, whatever blows your frock up pal, see you...*

PART 2 (HISTORY)

Venus is often called earth's twin planet, this is due to similarities in size and density.

The similarities end abruptly with temperature. With an average surface temperature of 400°C, it's not a place that had been considered for exploration-that is up until project Grosvenor. Materials that can withstand extreme temperatures had been developed years prior to the project; however where the BSP's triumph lay was in the development of material that could not only withstand temperatures exceeding 500°C, but could also safely house and protect human life under its surface. With this material perfected, Grosvenor went forward. Astral Engineers were able to chip away beneath the volcanic surface of the uninhabited planet, from their 4 man air-conditioned pods a full 40 metres from ground level.

It was from one of these pods that Richard Lloyd stumbled upon the element.

Electrical power is usually generated by electro-mechanical generators driven by steam produced from fossil fuel combustion, or the heat released from nuclear reactions; or from other sources such as kinetic energy extracted from wind or flowing water. It was Cleaver who managed to channel the powerful but sporadic and unstable energy emitting from Niroplaxia Gamonite, allowing it to act as a generator. Other physicists working on it knew that it was powerful, but saw it as dangerous and incompatible with Earth's atmosphere. Upon working out how to harness and subdue the element's stronger surges, Cleaver then needed a constant sympathetic environment in which to house it. He needed an immovable object to cancel out this unstoppable force, and so the Portentis Engine came into being.

Made from a criss-cross mesh of Tungsten and Titanium alloys, the Portentis Engine was developed by a team of ten- five scientists and five engineers- however the only names that were ever mentioned in the same breath as the world changing machine were Richard Lloyd, Ezekiel Cleaver, William Foxworthy, and Vincent Gwiazda. The rest of that team could feel especially aggrieved by the inclusion of Gwiazda, as he wasn't at all involved with the development of the Portentis Engine, his involvement was purely financial.

Part 3 (Press Conference)

Conference room C was already crowded when Helen Clyne arrived; she guessed half of the crowd consisted of over-zealous newbies and the others were just enjoying the rare chance to step inside the mysterious Sanhedrin, as if they were kids on a school trip.

The opportunity to see in the flesh and possibly even catch a word with the man himself was one that no self-respecting reporter would dream of passing up.

As she negotiated her way through the rabble to her seat fifth row from front, she couldn't help but feel slightly indignant at her positioning; she was Helen Clyne, crack journalist for one of the most reputable scientific publications in the country. She thought to herself haughtily "the very fact that I've been cast a full 3 rows behind *The Express* and *The Mail* speaks volumes about modern society." Dr Cleaver was a figure that had captured Helen's imagination as a teenager and he had continued to be a constant source of intrigue. Now in his late fifties, he still cut a striking figure. 6'1" in height with a strong jaw and piercing hazel eyes, his salt and pepper hair was always immaculately trimmed and his dark Caribbean skin simply refused to wither. Although good looking in an unassuming way, Cleaver's looks weren't the source of Clyne's infatuation. Cleaver oozed power, a diagnosis that had caused considerable sniggers when she first coined it at a dinner party a few years back. It wasn't even the fact that he was one the richest men on the planet.

The power that had held Clyne magnetised after all these years was somehow radiating from within the man. She had always found intelligence attractive, but this again was only a part of it.

As a couple of suits arrived and took their seats on the panel, Helen Clyne felt a pang of anticipation course though her. This was a monumental moment in her 12 year career; it wasn't just the sheer size of the story (it wasn't everyday three members of the public get murdered by Police Drones) it was also the first time Clyne was going to be in the presence of true greatness. Cleaver arrived and took his seat in the middle of his entourage of suits, the mumbling rabble became a frantic mess of voices, and the *rata tat* of multiple camera flashes produced a strobe effect upon their subject. Helen Clyne's heart raced. The sour faced man to Cleaver's right must have been his chosen legal eagle / spokesperson, Clyne guessed; he whispered a few things in his client's ear then rose.

"People, please can I have your attention!" The rabble settled. "Thank you, now we can either do this the easy way, in which you will quietly raise your hands and I pick who will get to ask a question, or we can do this the hard way, in which you become a frantic cacophony and my client and I simply get up and leave." The reality was somewhere in the middle. Helen Clyne had a thousand questions she longed to ask Dr Cleaver. However, this was a lottery, and she knew she would be lucky to get just one question in. After much back and forth, Clyne had settled on five questions, with one a definite first.

"Dr Cleaver, is this the end of Com Cops?" "Mr Cleaver, have you made contact with the families of the victims?" Though both valid questions, Clyne grimaced at their horribly clichéd and tabloid nature. "Dr Cleaver, what now for your national rollout plans?" "Dr Cleaver, will any jobs be lost because of this?" *Not bad*, she thought. "Mr Cleaver is it true that the victims were especially targeted?"…*Idiot*.

Although Cleaver's answers were measured, Clyne sensed his vulnerability. Being an extremely private man, the Dr had literally never been trapped in this kind of bear pit before; given that this was partly because in a lengthy career, everything that Cleaver touched seem to become a success. Clyne felt a wave of sympathy for the great man.

"All units are in lock up for testing and all operation has been suspended until further notice"

"We are working day and night to bring you the answers to…"

"No there were absolutely no precursors to the incidents"

"Although I am willing to shoulder most the responsibility for this terrible tragedy, please don't forget the 17 years previous of immaculate service, also please bear in mind the amount of murder and violent crime my drones have prevented"" No I am not making light of…please… one at a time!"

After what felt like an age, the sour faced man's beady eyes finally locked with hers, Helen Clyne's heart skipped a beat. "Yes, you there, the lady in the black blazer". Clyne looked at Cleaver, licked her lips and cleared her throat. "Dr Cleaver, Helen Clyne, *Science Journal UK*, can I just say I am a lifelong follower and admirer of your work". "Thank you", Cleaver's eyes visibly soften and a subtle smile along with an air of relief marked the scientist's face. Clyne remained stoic, "Dr Cleaver, what do these recent events mean for the Commissars?"

Cleaver's face dropped. The room fell silent.

PART 4 (DAX/BAXTER)

Felix Baxter was hunched over Andrew Dax's desk in the corner of his office, although Dax would tell you that it was no more than a glorified call centre cubicle.

"The pattern of the data irregularities are definitely in sync with the surges coming from Portentis," mumbled Baxter.

As Dax looked down on Baxter, crouching over the roll of readings almost in the foetal position, his greyish pallor, his brow glistening with sweat, the crack and wobble in the desperate engineer's voice, Dax thought to himself "my word it sucks to be you right now!" Felix Baxter had started his meeting with Dax admitting that his position would become vacant very soon if he couldn't find a passable reason why two of his machines had suddenly attacked three innocent people whilst on regulation patrol.

"Felix, with all due respect, the only real readable reaction to the pulses from Portentis is the odd power surge around the city, and, admittedly more unsettling, the big pulse a couple weeks ago. And I have it on good authority that the moles are looking into that. However, I really don't think any of this is connected to the Drone murders."

Baxter shot up from the swivel chair "DON'T FUCKING CALL THEM THAT!" he bellowed. "My units are not capable of "murder", humans murder, my units malfunction because of an error, and believe me, a human IS responsible for this," hissed the engineer, bringing his face a little closer to Dax's than he might have liked. "Hey!" snapped Dax, "Now this is before my time, but when the CCC was putting out its first proposals for taking over the force, wasn't it you that stated that CLEDs were all programmed exactly the same, by you, eradicating the possibility of public danger, and that the only break down that could possibly occur was mechanical?"

Baxter stared at Dax, his eyes glistening "I... I just can't..." Dax continued, softening his tone, as he sensed that the man before him was close to desperate tears.

"Listen Felix, what I was going to say was that, when I heard you say that, all those years ago on a news report, I never really bought it." Felix frowned, "I mean wasn't it Dr Cleaver himself that stated "There is no such thing as an exact science" Baxter reasoned, "But this isn't science, this is mechanics, electronic....engineering, my Drones cannot purposefully attack any more than that keyboard on your desk can grab a hold of your throat and start choking you!" Baxter paused and looked out of the window onto the city. "I was so careful".

Dax was never overly keen on Felix Baxter. This was mainly because, as Cleaver's right hand man, he would look down on all the other staff; Dax himself had been on the receiving end of the odd flippant remark. However, what Dax was witnessing before him now, Baxter standing slumped shouldered at the window in the corner of his office, staring out, was the flip side to this honour; he couldn't help but feel a little sorry for his shrivelled colleague.

"Felix, I am sorry I can't help you further, and I really

believe you had the absolute best intentions when producing these things." Dax walked over to Baxter and lowered his voice, "but my gut instinct back then, remains the same to this day, machines have no place in mankind's justice system."

PART 5

ANDREW DAX (BLOG ENTRY)

I'm fully aware that this therapeutic exercise was meant to be a blog of my life and not just work updates, and I will try to get off the subject soon, but things have been getting really weird down at the cop shop!

I've had Felix Baxter, (he's in charge of all things CLED, by the way) in my oversized cubicle, in a panic of pant-browning proportions. He's convinced the CLED incidents were in some way connected to the irregular data readings I had been receiving from the Portentis Engine. However, I think he was just clutching at straws, because his job's about as safe as eating your dinner off the floor of one the public toilets in Hyde Park.

That's not the only strange thing that's been going on around here. CCC has a new ad campaign; I know this purely because I keep seeing the posters around the city. There are a few different ones, but none of them give much away, just a couple of sentences and slogans, for example "**CONFIRMING LAW & ORDER WITH 2 GUNS**" in bold capital type, white on black - a little heavy handed I feel, but whatever. The only indication that this is one of our campaigns is the tiny logo in the bottom right hand corner. London's police force is part of a commercial conglomerate; and, although this has been the case for ages now, I still struggle with the concept at times. Especially being part of what some call the "crossover" generation.

The billboard that sticks out in my mind most is the one at the Canning Town stop where I catch my train to work. It simply reads:-

60%-NATURAL
40%-PRESICION-ENGINEERED
100% LAW ENFORCEMENT

Now apart from the obvious wrong maths, there is something inherently unnerving about this one.

One of the oddest occurrences of the last couple weeks though has to be the letter I got from work. Receiving a letter from your employer informing you that the company was scheduled to shut down the following week Monday through Wednesday, but confirming pay would remain unchanged, would please most. Not me though. It was too random, too ill-explained. Companies the size of CCC and Portentis Power which hold responsibility for both public safety and power for large chunks of a city cannot just shut down for 3 days.

After a few half-hearted attempts at gaining more information (the half-hearted nature of the attempts were more due to the expectation of failure than that of laziness) I gave in and, upon the advice of a colleague, "just fucking relaxed and enjoyed the break!"

People were talking alright, however they were talking about what they would do with their extra-long weekend, either that or pondering the complexities of whether to book the remaining 2 days off in order to gain a bonus week's holiday.

The moles have been scurrying around above ground

level a little too much since the big pulse. "Mole" is the in-work nickname given to the technicians that monitor and maintain the Portentis Engine. The fact that the engine electrically powers around half of the city, is one that keeps the moles pretty busy. They work separate hours, they have a separate entrance/exit and never really venture up as far as ground level. All these are contributory factors in the award of the moniker.

Over the last couple of weeks, more and more moles have been surfacing, zipping around with an air of urgency that I for one find as odd as I do disconcerting. I know their profile has been substantially raised of late, due to the pulse that shook the building a month prior, but for me, the drone executions, the weird readings and the big pulse along with that strange and forebodingly cryptic ad campaign all smell a little off. Rodger "the tool" tells me the company will go "daan the shitta" within 5 years, due to the CLED incidents. He reckons he knew one of the victims, but only from drinking in the same bars. He seemed to take a sick satisfaction in telling me how "the guy had the life literally squeezed out of him."

The regional and national rags back this up, apparently the guy was walking home drunk from a club, when the drone grabbed him by the shoulders and slowly "compressed" him to the extent that, when found, his torso was nothing more than a bag of blood, bone fragments and ruptured organs. Worst of all, the coroner's report says that the ordeal would have lasted a good (well, not "good") ten minutes…horrendous! Rodger has repeated that fact to me more than once, however he validates this with a bland sympathy, usually a variation of "poor sod" or the old classic "makes you think, don't it?"

Well Rodger, yes it does make me think actually! In fact, of the two, this was the story that had the most impact on me. I know, I know, a kid got shot dead in the other, and that's truly awful. However, whether it's the fact that the doomed party boy was around my age, or the seemingly purposefully sadistic nature of the incident, I'm not too sure, but it really bugs me.

Part 6 (Drone Patrol)

The Computerized Law Enforcement Drone (Com Cop or CLED) is a state of the art piece of electro-mechanical machinery whose design draws on the original concept popularised by Cleaver Corp's maiden project the Total Security Drone. The TSD was utilised for private and corporate security by large blue-chip companies situated largely in the US and UAE.

The Com Cop's main function is to provide support to any given manned law enforcement organisation. This support mainly consists of subduing violent or anti-social behaviour including riot control, and "Perp Pursuit".

Most of its operational functionality is programmed in before deployment on a job to job basis. However, it does have a range of pre-programmed intuitively triggered jobs for example "Conflict Subjugation" and the GPS controlled "Direct Arrest" command.

The machine garners the derogatory nickname "Dalek" or "Road Sweeper" – the latter is due to its similarities in size and shape, plus the sound that it emits when hovering.

It has two separate hover heights, "Regular Patrol" which is 40 centimetres from surface level and "Pursuit" at a full 16 ft. in the air. This is high enough not to interfere with regular traffic but low enough to follow any given road route. It can glide at a top speed of 50 mph; this can only be achieved in "Hot Pursuit" mode. The unit also comes complete with a range of pre-recorded voice commands including "STOP, POLICE!" and "ADHERENCE IS OBLIGATORY".

Each Com Cop boasts twin ferrying compartments and can comfortably ferry two, seated adult arrestees at any one time. They also have four hydraulic apprehension arms: two of which intuitively compress the arrestee just enough to immobilise them, the other two are weaponised.

50 units have been operational predominantly around Central and East London for the last 17 years.

3

PART 1 (EZEKIEL CLEAVER)

W*ho in god's name is Helen Clyne, and how the hell does she know about the Commissars?* Cleaver questioned himself, sitting cue in hand on one of his oversized oxblood leather chairs.

Some years back, following a bout of severe headaches that his personal physician attributed to stress; one of Cleaver's "close men" had advised Cleaver to install a games room. "You need somewhere to unwind", he was told. And so there Cleaver sat, at the head of his pool table, in the pre-approved game room of his Hertfordshire mansion, decidedly stressed.

At the time that Clyne had questioned Cleaver regarding the Commissars, it had completely thrown him. Cleaver had felt that he had relative control of the press conference up until this stage. At the time he was so shaken that all he could muster was stuttering denial, "Commissars, what is that? I'm sorry I don't follow"etc.. Not even Cleaver himself found this performance convincing. He kept rerunning the moment in his mind, *they all knew, they must have.* On numerous occasions, Cleaver had attempted to reanimate his initial facial reaction to the question put to him. Unfortunately, this only served to confirm his initial conclusion His instant reaction was pure and had clearly betrayed his lie.

What followed was one of the strangest verbal exchanges Cleaver had ever been involved in. It was almost as if Clyne sensed his vulnerability and wished to dangle him for a while. However, she didn't wish to unmask him fully. He got the feeling she held back much of what she had somehow discovered, and that the main objective of her cryptic questioning was to let Cleaver, and only Cleaver know, that she was privy to his covert plans.

Ezekiel Cleaver was a meticulously private person and this filtered into his work. There were only a handful of people who knew about the Commissars, and they had signed an agreement which swore them to secrecy. The robustness of the document ensured that only the most frivolous of individuals would be foolish enough to breach the agreement. Cleaver didn't surround himself with frivolous men.

"We need to do something about that bitch, she's dangerous!" Cleaver recalled Felix Baxter's venomous words. Although the scientist was unquestionably in charge, it was Baxter who seemed to harbour a considerable aggressive side. Cleaver himself was no shrinking violet when it came to testing the flexibility of the rules but there was an almost manic ferocity fuelling Baxter's words that Cleaver found a little concerning. Cleaver had noticed this one other time during their working relationship.

Although Cleaver was more than a little unsettled by Baxter's words, he couldn't escape the fact that he needed Felix Baxter more now than at any other time in their relationship, he also knew that there was no way he could hold the Engineer to the one week deadline he had flung at him in the heat of the moment. Indeed, the deadline had already passed.

The Helen Clyne problem was an unquestionably big one; however it was dwarfed when placed beside the conundrum of maintaining city law and order sans Drones. Things had already started to take an ugly turn, with two Walthamstow Reg-Ops Officers (formerly Police Constables) kicked half to death already. That hadn't happened in almost a decade. Cleaver knew you couldn't change the core of humanity by simply installing a more uncompromising method of policing. It was as if the truly committed monsters out there were simply lying in wait, with an unshakable, almost religious faith that they would again have their day, eventually.

The notion of keeping any of the Drones online and operational was out of the question. The grim fact was that the Sanhedrin CCC, London's only source of law and order, had to run at a mere 60% capacity for the foreseeable future. The thought of going crawling to the military for support, as suggested by the Prime Minister, turned the Dr's stomach. His relationship with the British Military had been a strained one. Cleaver would tell you that this was because of their "preposterous arrogance."

It had already been decided that the deployment of Abercrombie and Sark would be brought forward. Although he was facing unarguably the toughest challenge of his working life, Cleaver couldn't help but feel a tinge of excitement when thinking about his two new charges. Cleaver Corp as an umbrella organisation was multifaceted and had several businesses and product services, which were effortlessly able to run independently of each other. However Abercrombie and Sark were his personal vision. In fact, Cleaver had not felt this proud of a project since his "first born" – the Total Security Drone, all those years ago.

At that time, Cleaver being a physicist, left production and what he called the nuts and bolts in the capable hands of William Foxworthy and co, however the design and overall vision was solely Cleaver's.

His two new favourite people could easily pick up 20% of the slack left by the Drones. Abercrombie and Sark were presently the only two people left in Cleaver's life that he really felt he could trust.

"Those two boys are going to change everything," he assured himself.

PART 2 (ROB & HELEN CLYNE)

It was Mexican night. Rob Clyne always looked forward to tonight.

Up until the last 18 months or so, Mexican night would occur every week. However, of late, because of his maddeningly driven sister's work programme, the tradition had been diluted down to a once monthly event.

Rob and Helen had always been close as siblings, despite being very different creatures. Rob was twenty-six and, by his own admission, a "serial temp", who had made his way through most of the warehouses and storage units that the city had to offer. He wasn't lazy by any means, in fact he was well known throughout the temp recruitment world for his speed and efficiency, and was rarely without a contract. He just wasn't a career man. Helen, on the other hand, was three years his senior and had wanted to be a journalist since the age of 12.

As they took their seats at their regular window table at Casa Vasquez, the waiter was already approaching them, smiling in recognition. Rob ordered a beer, Helen, a glass of dry white. They went for their usual, El' Mexicano Classico, which consisted of tacos and fajitas, along with a plethora of sides, salads and other delights. There were two other Mexican themed restaurants in the relative locality but Helen and Rob always chose Vasquez. The fact that it was a standalone and not a chain gave it a more authentic feel. Plus it came without the loud and horribly on-the-nose stock Latino music.

The music in Casa Vasquez was subtle and gentle, often consisting of nothing but naked flamenco guitar. There were no speakers protruding from the outside walls, imploring passers-by to come and join the celebración, and, most importantly, the food was exceptional.

"So you're still alive then?" Rob said wryly. Helen rolled her eyes.

When his sister had a big story to cover, especially one this close to her heart, it consumed her. Rob had, on more than one occasion, expressed his concern with this particular project.

"So how did "Dr Play-God" react to your questions? You said you got a couple in didn't you?" Helen shook off her raincoat, "Your nicknames are shit, and your wit is snail-paced, you know that right?"

"Yep" her brother confirmed.

Helen was a fearless journalist. She didn't mind getting her hands dirty or indeed putting her own personal safety at considerable risk, for the good of the story.

Her theory was "Our lives are ending one day at a time, regardless of our actions, I just want mine to end with the blood rushing through my veins whilst doing something I have a genuine passion for, is that so crazy?"

She had been told on countless occasions what an outstanding tabloid columnist she would have made, not to mention a considerably richer columnist at that. However, the thought of selling her soul to tabloid journalism made Helen's skin crawl.

Her lust for the story was matched equally by an insatiable thirst for knowledge. Intellectual journalism was the obvious compromise.

Her brother hated what he called Cleaver's London. He stated on more than one occasion that "no one man should hold that much power", and confirmed it would "all end in tears". Why he didn't just leave London, Helen could never understand. He'd even opted out of signing up to Portentis Power, in favour of a more expensive tariff.

Helen loved her brother dearly but felt he could be so melodramatic at times.

She continued "Well, needless to say, I rendered him speechless."

Rob smirked, "Course he couldn't speak, your stare turned him to stone!"

"Shut up," Helen laughed.

Rob Clyne lowered his smile, "seriously sis I know how you feel about Cleaver and all that, but whatever big conspiracy you've uncovered, I genuinely think you should keep it to yourself this time. Someone that powerful isn't to be toyed with, we're mere mortals remember!"

"Who said anything about a conspiracy?" Helen wanted to change the subject. They both had such differing views on Cleaver Corp and all it stood for, that it had led to arguments in the past. The last thing she wanted to do was sour the evening with that tired debate, especially since she had cancelled on him last month. "Anyway, you still at City Express, or have you moved on again? You big agency whore!" But Rob persevered. "Seriously sis, you keep snooping around an organisation as scary as the Corp and you may end up "disappearing"". Helen frowned, "stop it", "Ahh Come on, gotta be extra careful where you tread these days, remember Richard Lloyd? You can't possibly believe that Cleaver had nothing to do with that!"

"Robbie, please, let's not do this again," Helen pleaded.

"Fine" Rob slumped in his seat childishly and smirked. "But you know you've missed your first and only chance to pop the question to the OAP of your dreams".

Helen sipped her wine, "who said I missed my chance? I was gonna ask you to be ring bearer."

Rob rolled his eyes, "Yeah, yeah".

The remainder of their evening was as standard, reminiscing, whilst sipping perfectly chilled beer and wine. They would explore the full spectrum of laughter from "snigger" through to "full belly" often muffled under mouthfuls of perfectly seasoned chicken and pillow-soft fresh tortilla.

As they paid their bill plus a generous tip, Rob provided their regular waiter with his joke of the month. With each visit, Rob would have a new joke for the young Spaniard (there weren't enough genuine Mexicans around East London to fill the quota). However his grasp of the English language was limited. The pair knew very well that their waiter very rarely understood what was being said, however he would judge when the punch line would land, then laugh heartily. His manically over the top guffawing would in turn send the tipsy siblings off on their own journey into genuine hysterics, and so it went on.

As they stepped out into the brisk evening, Rob seemed restless, "lets pop into the New Inn for a quick one before we get the tube." Helen frowned and wobbled slightly. "I've had enough I think." Rob jogged ahead of her impatiently, and then turned to face her, now walking backwards. "Oh come on grandma! It's well early, and besides we'll pass it on the way."

Rob continued speaking, but Helen couldn't hear the rest of his sentence. Although her eyes were locked with her brother's, she couldn't make out his words. Rob obviously shared this sensation, as he frowned and inserted his left index finger into his ear and turned it back and forth.

Just then Helen realised that it wasn't just her brother's words which she was unable to fathom; the world had gone silent, as if she'd been cast into water. She opened her mouth to speak. Suddenly, Rob's eyebrows rose in alarm, he slowly looked down at his feet. Helen felt pressure building in her ears. She took a step towards her brother, and then hesitated.

Rob grabbed his stomach; his head bolted up to meet her gaze once again, his eyes bulged with panic and fear, his mouth gaping in a silent scream. His expression filled Helen with a dread that was so complete, she was convinced that these were her final few moments.

She cried out "what the hell's happening, Rob?" but her words were inaudible. Rob was now convulsing, scarlet blood began to pour from both nostrils. In a state of shock, Helen stumbled towards her brother, but as she touched him she was knocked backwards by what felt like a powerful electric shock, she stumbled and fell backwards onto the concrete, the small of her back taking the brunt of the impact. A flare of pain leapt up her spine from her coccyx.

Panicked tears blurred her vision for a moment, as she groped around desperately trying to get back to her feet. Her eyes cleared and she looked up at her beloved brother, his feet were planted, while his upper body thrashed around frantically, pulses of blood spraying up and out into the night air, his eyes rolled back in his skull to the extent that his pupils were no longer visible. She was so confused and afraid that she felt a noxious pool of bile begin to physically bubble within her gut.

Helen Clyne was screaming, she was screaming so hard that she tasted blood and her lungs burned as if ablaze.

Someone approached her from the right and grabbed her shoulder. Still being deaf, she jumped in surprise; the stranger was actually helping her to her feet. As she stood she didn't even attempt turning to identify her helper, Helen started towards her brother, but as she did, another impact battered her. This one's effect would prove to be permanent.

Part 3 (Tom Cartwright)

"Yes! I've nailed it, I've friggin' nailed it!" cried Officer Tom Cartwright across the Central Enforcements office. Central Enforcements was the collective name of the remaining manned police force and administration, situated at the back of the Sanhedrin complex.

For the last six months, Cartwright had been working on the "Wolf" case, tirelessly monitoring the five main players. The city's more heavy handed criminal violations such as assault, armed robbery and antisocial behaviour had all been minimised, however organized crime was still rife. Wolf was the biggest people and drug trafficking syndicate in the country. Their operations were Europe-wide and tight as a drum, running the gamut from child prostitution to class A narcotic smuggling.

The five core members of Wolf were ghosts; it had been this way for the last 4 years or so. CLEDs, although robust, were rendered quite useless when it came to outsmarting a slick operation of this calibre. CLEDs were created to be peacekeepers in a primitive sense. A few detectives had attempted but eventually failed to snag all five in one swoop, instead submitting to tracking them from city to city. As he raced across the office, Cartwright was reminded of how the Chief had put it best a few years ago: "the bastards are like liquid, you just can't get hold of em!" The young officer, after much pleading, had been offered an opportunity to have a go at catching the five together, and in the act. The Chief had authorised this purely because, although he liked and saw potential in the young officer, he knew the venture would ultimately end up exactly how it had done historically, in frustrated failure.

However Tom Cartwright had not only gained confirmation of a meeting between the five, but this meeting was to take place tonight, in London!

"CHIEF!" Cartwright forgot himself as he burst into Walt Robson's office, almost falling in. Robson was on the phone, "WHAT THE FU…" He jolted in surprise and glared up at Cartwright. The glare aided Cartwright in remembering his station; he grimaced in apology and tried to remain quiet until the conclusion of his boss' phone call.

"What is it Tom? I'm up to my eyeballs, so it wants to be important!"

When Cartwright went on to explain his discovery, Chief Robson refused to believe it at first. However, as they hunched over Cartwright's desk, watching the play back of what the officer had captured, the Chief raised his head slowly and stared at Cartwright. "This is very, very nice work son, at worst we'll get closer than we ever have done, at best… well, we'll have the bastards, ALL OF 'EM!" He laughed out loud and slapped the young officer on the shoulder.

Almost inevitably, Officer Cartwright's high was about to take a spectacular nose dive. The chief had disappeared back into his office to make contact with the directorate. Upon his return he went on to explain to Tom that he was not permitted to be present at the pick-up operation.

"But I'm a bloody Ops Officer!, This is what I was trained to do! Please Chief, don't stiff me on this one!" pleaded Cartwright.

"Look son, I feel for you, I really do, but it's already been decided. Besides, no one's really getting to go. Abercrombie and Sark only on this one and that's an order direct from the top. It's sort of their maiden voyage."

"This stinks sir, this stinks to high heaven and you can't

tell me it doesn't." Cartwright had always felt that police work should be done by police. However the title of Chief of Police, he felt, was constantly being undermined by decisions made by a businessman. Cartwright resented this deeply.

"We're being phased out, aren't we Chief?"

"Stop being so bloody melodramatic Tommy". Chief Robson had to play the allegation down, however this very same notion had caused him more than one sleepless night in the recent past. "If this thing goes off right, you get to be Billy big bollocks; no one's taking that from you, for god's sake you should be happy! There's less chance of getting killed this way."

"With all due respect sir, how can I be happy? I mean, they aren't even real coppers are they?" Cartwright paused, "in fact they're the exact opposite." He lowered his voice to almost a whisper and looked his boss in the eye, "you can't honestly tell me you're happy about this, sir?" They stared at each other in silence. Robson sighed heavily. "Listen, happy or not, this is the way things are going now. It's not as if it's been all of a sudden, now has it? The way the suits upstairs see it, is that they're protecting us." Cartwright frowned and opened his mouth to speak, but Robson continued. "Look, there's nothing I can say to make this easier to swallow, and I will admit that the days of the beat bobby do seem numbered. However I will say this, there will always be a place in this game for smart coppers like you Tommy."

"Always."

1 ANDREW DAX (BLOG ENTRY)

I t's been 4 weeks since "Pulse/Drone-kill", and I have to admit, I really ain't loving this place anymore.

There are the power cuts which to be honest are more of an annoyance than anything. However I fear they are a much more than that to the company itself.

What I cannot abide are the heat and the weird ears!

You know that feeling I mentioned in an earlier update, where I said you get that ear popping thing when you venture down too close the moles' lair? Well it's happening to everyone in the building at the moment, and with more frequency. It was strange. "Social study" strange. By this I mean that the symptom wasn't picked up as a building issue for a good while. This was because for the first 2 weeks or so, everyone thought it was their problem alone. I mean think about it, if you were at work and the colleague next to you says "man, my ears keep blocking up, then popping, it hurts a bit too", then conversely you had the same physical anomaly the next day, would you immedi- ately think "my god this building is trying to sabotage one of our primary senses, everybody OUT NOW, EVERY

MAN FOR HIMSELF!!'"? No, nor did most employees of Cleaver Corp.

It wasn't until one of the moles down stairs apparently started projectile vomiting and then passed out, that people rightly or wrongly made a connection and word started to circulate. Eventually everyone realised almost as one, that the problem only occurred when they were at work, along with the fact that they weren't alone.

All we are getting from upstairs is that it's some kind of "air pressure problem" and although it causes "minor discomfort" there is no risk of serious harm. I am not so sure. Although I don't believe Portentis is somehow commanding drones to kill, via some kind of weird tele-kinetic binary, I do think there is something going on down there. Then there's the heat, the bloody unbearable heat! No one can seem to figure out where it's coming from. The centralised heating system was shut off weeks ago, which had to be done manually, as its winter, but still there's this horrible heat. The problem must be serious, because I've seen not only moles, but outside contractors scaling the interior and exterior walls of the building, brandishing elaborate tools and scanning devices. It struck me that in my six years here, until now, I had never, ever seen any outside contractor set foot in the Sanhedrin.

The most open I've seen the building was at the post drone-kill press conference, but I guess that was kind of unavoidable.

Also, I keep seeing these two creepy-ass guys around the site.

The first time I saw them, I guessed they were just another pair of nameless, faceless hired goons that scan us glumly at reception. You know the type; they're usually instantly forgettable, right? However, I've seen this pair outside the entrance to sub cellar (that's where Portentis lives). Then, at another time, they were guarding an entrance at each end of the computer room. Security has always been tight around the huge complex- it has to be- however I can't remember ever seeing the computer room being guarded in this way. I mean it's a computer room for heaven's sake! The name alone should put off the most optimistic thrill seeker, and it's not even as if the computers in this particular room hold any juicy secrets or conspiracies. It's not as if you're going to walk in, tap around on a machine picked at random, then walk out with a copied photo of Cleaver passionately frenching the Prime Minister or anything (now I'm not say this hasn't happened mind, but just confirming that you won't find footage of it in this particular room).

These things basically take readings, shake them up a little then send them somewhere else, that's it! The only people these readings make any sense to are horribly dull people like me.

There's something definitely amiss with these two though.

At this point you may be thinking "Andrew Dax, serial dissector of the mundane, strikes again," and granted I have difficulty explaining myself on this subject, but I have a real gut feeling about this. Firstly, I've never heard them speak, not to each other, not to anyone. Also, you know that expression "dead behind the eyes?" Well, this doesn't quite do these two goons justice. Somehow their eyes don't seem real; expressionless is one thing, but being void of even basic signals of reaction or recognition is something else entirely.

The day I went up to check out something patently uninteresting in the computer room and stumbled upon the larger but decidedly less creepy of the duo, is a day I will never forget.

I spotted him upon my approach; and gave him the obligatory half smile and quick nod. He just stared through me. I slowed; he took a step forward blocking my entrance. I looked up at him, awaiting instruction…nothing. At a glimpse, he was regulation bouncer fare; black, skin-headed, 6'6" at least and built like a semi-detached. I gave it something lame like "erm…just need to check on…" then pointed around him. As I motioned to pass him, immediately a large sinewy hand was on my shoulder, I swear I didn't even see it rise! But that wasn't what alarmed me, and indeed will continue to haunt me for many a year.

The hand was cold.

The hand was so cold that the chill instantly penetrated my jumper and shirt, and within seconds it was sending a dull ache trickling through my shoulder into my chest. I visibly shuddered. Then I remembered myself and tried to mask my reaction to the frightening sensation. He raised his other hand to reveal an LCD electronic tablet sign, which read *CLEARANCE MUST BE PROVIDED TO ENTER THIS AREA.* As I looked beyond him, it became apparent that the door's access control was on the fritz. I looked back at "Mr Personality" and wasn't sure whether to check his pulse, as his face hadn't moved. He was wearing a long, black double-breasted coat, which looked like a wool mix. Nice look, if you ignore the two obvious bulges that were visible on each hip. Why the hell would a security guard, commissioned outside the computer room need to be armed?

I showed him my clearance. He took it from me, and for the first time in our brief encounter, his eyes seemed to focus. He stared at my pass intently for what seemed like an age. As he handed my pass back to me, the hand left my shoulder, which was a relief as the ache had become moderate pain. He stepped aside.

"What the hell was that?" I thought to myself, shuddering again, as the door slid open and I passed the threshold.

PART 6

Destination: Clayton's Steel Mill (Abandoned) – SE7
    Objective: Collect 5 persons
    Environment: Hostile
    Force: Moderate
    Weaponry Type: N/A
    Vehicle: Private Ambulance (Cover)
    Driver: Jason Sark
    Time of departure: 22:00
    Estimated time of return: 22:50

Part 3(Dax/Clyne)

"Excuse me, are you Andrew Dax?" The voice was female.

Dax couldn't remember the last time he'd been approached by a female in a bar, a female he didn't know that was. He didn't recognise the voice but he knew who it was before he turned around. "Yeah that's me, do I know you?" Dax enquired. He had noticed a woman had been staring at him intermittently from a couple of tables away earlier on that night. She was attractive, but not stunning, and only stood out because she was alone. "She's definitely looking at you geez, but it don't seem particularly positive, in fact I think she's giving you evils! I reckon you know her but don't remember how" proclaimed Danny Adams, Adams was Dax's childhood friend. Danny had just left, and Dax having just sunk the last of his bottle was also about to leave Jay's Bar, which was situated a few streets from the Sanhedrin.

"You're a systems analyst at the CCC, aren't you?" "Erm, data analyst, yes," Dax corrected, then furrowed his eyebrows. "I am sorry, I don't mean to be rude, you seem to know me, but I can't place you at all".

"My name is Helen Clyne."

Dax recognised the name immediately, his stomach churned. He'd been hearing her name around work a lot in the weeks that followed the press conference over in C, the press conference that prompted a strict gagging order for all staff on pain of sacking and even arrest.

Apparently, Clyne was the reporter who had stumped his boss with her questioning. Dax figured, if she could render a man of Cleaver's intellect speechless, then he stood absolutely no chance! "I'm sorry; I can't talk to the press. I'm not a crusader or anything; I'm just a bloke trying to remain employed." Dax said briskly, but Clyne persevered, "no, no, you don't understand, it isn't…." Dax was desperate to make an escape, unscathed. "Miss, I'm sorry, even if I could speak to you, I really don't know anything, honestly! Now I've really got to run".

He shrugged on his jacket and turned to leave, just then he felt a hand grab his arm. "STOP PLEASE!" Helen Clyne cried out, drawing far more attention than

Dax would have liked. He halted and turned. The woman's eyes were glistening with tears, her expression was haunted. Dax realised that the desperation in this woman's voice was genuine.

PART 7

It had been just over three weeks since Helen Clyne had lost her brother.

Although he had been rushed to Accident and Emergency, Helen knew she had witnessed the moment that Robert Jonathan Clyne's life had been extinguished. The cry that pierced the air that night, just yards from Casa Vasquez, where the axis of merriment and despair was so suddenly tipped, was a sound that would leave an indelible scar on her heart. In a twist of cruel irony, the impact of her brother's scream had been intensified by the fact that Helen's hearing had suddenly returned to her, just in time for her to hear it.

The coroner would tell Helen and her family that Rob's substantial internal injuries were caused by a powerful electric shock, originating from an underground power surge. They would then go on to provide "comfort" by confirming that this was a very rare occurrence, and that Rob was simply part of an unfortunate minority.

"I am so sorry for your loss, I really am, but you'll have

to forgive me, I'm trying to work out how this is connected to me." Dax tried to keep his tone sympathetic, "Are you suggesting that what happened to your brother is somehow connected to the CCC?" Dax leaned in closer; they had taken the precaution of moving to a table in the corner of Jay's and lowering their voices. "Cos if that's the case, I genuinely don't feel I'm the right person to be quizzing. The very fact that you know who I am means you probably know more about my company than I do".

Helen stared at Dax for a moment, as if trying to assort her words "I used to read your blog."Dax raised his eyebrows.

Andrew Dax, the self-titled non-computer enthusiast, had once been the sole proprietor of an online IT helpdesk, from which he would provide free basic IT advice for all who needed it. At least it had started life as this, but before long it became more of a forum for general tech discussion. At this stage, Dax became more of a mediator than anything. Dax would post a general tech blog daily, it would usually consist of his theories and predictions for upcoming technology, and this would always spark the forum into motion. It was these forecasts, delivered in perfect deadpan that had first caught Helen Clyne's attention.

Although Helen enjoyed Dax's writing, and often found herself laughing out loud at his quips, it wasn't the style of his prose that kept Helen coming back, it was the fact that the man was always right!

Every prediction- from kit and systems to trends and sales- came to pass. Even his most "in the know" detractors were eventually silenced by Dax's idiot savant- style gift. Helen had started to trust Dax's musings so much that on occasion she would even use him as a source for her own writing.

Dax would often mention his "face meltingly boring"

job; however he was always very careful to keep the CCC anonymous. However Clyne quickly deduced who the droll blogger's employer was. It wasn't just the fact that she had been a keen follower of all things Cleaver since her formative years, but also, she knew that the only way Dax could be privy to such accurate information regarding the technology development market, was to be close to the razor's edge, and you didn't get any closer than working under the Cleaver Corp umbrella.

"Wow, I haven't thought about that for a while! You really used to read that thing?" Dax smirked: "you don't look like a nerd". For the first time in their encounter, Helen's face cracked with a faint smile "Well looks can be deceiving, I write for *Science Journal UK*, so I have a sort of vested interest, besides you're a good writer." "No I'm not." Dax quickly corrected, frowning dismissively.

Helen looked around, the haunted look had returned to her visage. "The point is, I think what happened to Robbie is connected to Portentis Power, both on a basic level, because where we were situated that night, is over one of your grids," Dax squirmed uncomfortably at the ownership placed on him. Helen lowered her voice further, "but I also believe there may be something wrong with the actual source of the power itself." Dax was desperately trying to mask his unease, as he too had been harbouring concerns over the stability of the LC Element of late.

They stared at each other, as if trying to fathom the gravity of Clyne's theory. "Now, I don't know if this is relevant, but just before and during what happened that night, my ears blocked up and I felt an intense pressure building within my inner ear. Do you know anything or have you heard anything about this symptom around work at all?"

She continued. "The reason why I think its connected is because I'm sure Rob…" her voice wobbled with emotion, and she cut off. Helen shut her eyes tight, releasing a couple of bitter tears from each eye. She took a deep breath and tried to keep it together. "Sorry, what I was going to say was, I'm sure Robbie felt it too, just before he went." Dax gave his own exhale of submission, "Look, Helen I really would like to help you and if you weren't a reporter I would probably risk it but…" Clyne cut him off. "I'm being monitored." Dax frowned "By Central Enforcements." Dax jolted upright "What? You wait till now to tell me that? Oh god. Why me? Why have you chosen me to do this to?"

Helen felt a rush of resentment at Dax's slightly snivelling tone, "hey look, did I choose this?" Dax locked her gaze. "No I didn't. Sometimes, unfortunately, situations choose you" she hissed, "I've come to you because there *IS* no one else; I am not looking for a story I swear to you." Dax slumped in his seat. "Please, I am begging you, just hear me out. Besides I wasn't followed here so relax."

Dax didn't know why, but he felt drawn to this woman, it wasn't as much physical attraction, as an overwhelming sense of familiarity with this stranger, which he couldn't explain.

He sighed. "Ok, but not here."

4

The time is 10:17pm and a large black vehicle quietly prowls the desolate back streets on the outskirts of South East London.

Once a thriving industrial area, it is now an urban void. Sark and Abercrombie are the two men present in the front cab of the vehicle. Sark drives. They sit in silence. Abercrombie's eyes dart from left to right, as if watching a frantic rally in a tennis match. The only other movement in the cab is coming from Sark's leather gloved hands on the steering wheel, whilst he navigates the automatic vehicle. A large LED monitor takes up the majority of the central dashboard, upon which a constant flow of data frantically scroll. The large automobile lurches forward with an almost self-aware menace.

Street lights either haven't made it this far out on the fringes of the city, or they'd simply been decommissioned some years back.

The ink black vehicle, which is darker than the night, turns left onto what used to be a manufacturing industrial park, it crawls to a stop in a gully down to the right-hand side of a large abandoned unit.

Sark slowly shuts off the engine; the "plinck" of the cab's automatic internal light turning on is the only sound. Both men sit in perfect silence, bathed in the soft glow of the internal light. Both men's eyes dart left and right but no words are exchanged, both men face front, dead still. "Plinck" the cabs internal light fades, the two men sit in complete darkness for a few minutes. They both exit the vehicle in synchronized fashion. The two men walk boldly to the back of the complex to a large steel door with a closed viewing slot at eye level. Mumbled voices simmer from within. Both men stop and stand a few yards back as if hesitant, their eyes flickering back and forth, a cold tension laces the night air. Abercrombie, the smaller of the two, breaks his stance, approaches the door and raps firmly three times. *Bang, bang, bang!* The sound splits the night air like a hammer, the voices hush.

Part 2 (Ezekiel Cleaver)

How much loss can one person take, and still function?

The Cleaver Corp Empire was still in its infancy when Vincent Gwiazda committed suicide. It came as a massive shock, and not just to his family and friends, but to the business world as a whole. A hugely successful businessman who was just 48 years old, with an ex-model wife ten years his junior, and two healthy, intelligent teenage children, he was also halfway through a highly successful range of self – help business publications.

It was hard to understand why such a person would want to halt his own existence. One of the hardest hit by Vincent's passing was Ezekiel Cleaver himself. In fact, the scientist went into kind of depression after losing his business partner and closest friend. Those in close proximity had their theories. One of which was that he was filled with regret, as they hadn't spoken since a falling out just weeks before the incident. Others spoke of abandonment issues. Cleaver didn't have many friends, and Richard Lloyd had bailed on him some years before.

However, Ezekiel Cleaver was a self-made man. This isn't your run of the mill rags to riches story mind, Cleaver was a self-made man in its purest form. The youngest of three brothers and orphaned at the age of 11, with the remaining four members of his family wiped out in a car wreck. The headline that reads "WHOLE FAMILY KILLED IN HORROR CRASH!" didn't apply to the Cleaver's. This was because young Zeke was patiently waiting at a friend's house to be picked up for the weekly shopping trip on that fateful evening.

Whole family lost at age 11, best friend number one vanishes at age 33, best friend number 2 commits suicide at age 41. Who wouldn't feel a little abandoned? Cleaver had never married, either.

Losing everyone you hold dear isn't new or unique, however it does produce different reactions from person to person...

Cleaver simply decided to become the most important man on the planet.

Part 3 (Wolf)

The five core members of Wolf are standing in a dimly lit workshop space, having just finished their meeting regarding the shipment of 30 Serbian teenage girls into Soho, to begin their careers within the British underage sex trade.

At least two of the three Marsh brothers have topped the UK wanted list for nearly a decade. Micky Marsh is the oldest of the brothers and the founder member of Wolf. He is a smart and logical thinking criminal with a flair for the analytical.

Bobby "Pretty Boy" Marsh is the middle child and the face of the organisation's more commercially focussed operations. Robert Marsh is a cool, calculated customer with immaculate dress sense and shark- like instincts.

Tommy Marsh is the runt of the litter, and was literally taken on by Wolf to spare him from the death penalty. He is the group's metaphorical "dog on a leash"; his past exploits are frequently recited by other members; to threaten would-be whistle blowers into silence. Anyone tempted to take his slight stature as a weakness, should be immediately advised other-wise. Thomas Marsh is a dead-eyed sadist, with a crime sheet that would make Albert Anastasia nervous.

Jordi Van Hassel is a prominent figure in the under-ground sex industry across Europe, and his involvement in Wolf is strictly anonymous. The final big player is Vaughn McManus, a brash Bostonian expat. Vaughn is the logistics expert, what his countrymen would call a real "teamster". With an air of the delusional, Vaughn calls his part of the business the "clean" side.

"So it's settled, we pick up at Liverpool," Micky confirmed, meeting McManus's disapproving gaze. "Now I know you aint keen Macca, but trust me, anything south of the Watford Gap would be way too risky, even with the Daleks off the streets".

"SHHHH!" Bobby Marsh interrupted suddenly, the rest of the men frowned, as they had heard nothing, however they all hushed. Bobby stood frozen to the spot listening intently…silence. Micky rolled his eyes and continued "Anyway, we could just…"**BANG BANG BANG!**

The large steel door in the adjacent reception area boomed. All five men gasped in unison, frozen to the spot, wide eyed. "The law?" Tommy Marsh whispered.

"Impossible," Micky hissed. The men stood in silence staring at each other. The air was thick with tension.

"Well whoever it is, they're fucking dead now," Tommy proclaimed as he turned towards the reception area, unsheathing his Glock 18. "Tom, don't!" Micky admonished under his breath. Tommy ignored and strode confidently out of the room down the short hallway towards the steel door. Tommy Marsh expected protesting voices from the other side of the door. The lack of any sound made his swagger slow to a creep. The silence was deafening, at this point the whole group would have preferred another knock on the door to break the suffocating tension. "Oos out there?" Tommy waited for a response, he leaned in close to the door...nothing. The rest of the men were inching in behind the youngest Marsh, guns drawn.

He slowly slid the viewing panel open, and squinted as he tried to make out the source of the knock.

BOOM! Like a metallic explosion. The men jolted in surprise, as Tommy's limp body flew towards them. The youngest Marsh's small frame landed with a loose sounding *thud* before them, Bobby was first to look up and notice that the small rectangular slot in the door had tripled in size leaving a large, star-shaped hole. The four men still stood aghast, mouths gaping, guns drawn. The door swung open, and two men strolled boldly into the reception area. The leading man was white, ghostly pale and of medium height and build. The other was black, tall and built like a colossus. Both men were dressed in dark business suits under double breasted smart coats.

"You fuck!" cried McManus, who was the first to snap out of his shocked stupor. He squeezed of a round from his gun, the bullet seemed to clip Mr White's temple: open wound, no blood. The intruder halted his approach. McManus smirked as he waited for Mr White to either squeal in agony or fall to the floor. Mr White did neither, his blank expression was the last thing McManus would recall of the event.

Mr White took control of the situation; he cast off his coat, crouched low, leaning forward into McManus almost in one liquid movement.

SLAM! The swing happened too quickly to be visible; however McManus's head whipping back, along with an audible crunch, signalled that the Bostonian's defensive attempts had come to a close, he landed on top of Tommy.

Mr Black- the giant- stood back and let his associate enjoy himself. His pale faced partner glided smoothly in between the panicking group.

Everything slowed down and sped up at the same time.

BANG…**BANG**… a sound of the random gun fire of desperate and confused men, attempting to encircle their intruder. Mr White welcomed this, and slinked down to finish his work.

Head down… swing… **SMACK… CRUNCH…** a gun flew into the air. Jordie Van Hassel fell to his knees, already unconscious, mouth hanging open, jawbone protruding from his left cheek obscenely. A jet of blood exploded from his open face.

Jordie was out of the equation.

BANG…BANG

Head down…. swing…. **OOOFF!** The sound burst from Micky Marsh.

The impact again wasn't visible, but the way Micky quickly doubled over, alluded to a severe gut shot.

WHIP…. SLAM… CRUNCH

That sound again, like a walnut, giving in to a nutcracker. Micky Marsh jerked backwards, a wet gurgle spewed from him as he hit the deck.

Four men dispatched in less than 20 seconds. However, Robert Marsh was an experienced martial artist, and he began bouncing backwards on the balls of his feet, fists up, constantly moving, breathing in short, sharp bursts through his teeth. "Come on then…come on!" Bobby shouted, as he danced a semi-circle before his blank faced opponent, the wobble in his voice betraying the confidence in his combative words.

Pale face stood stoic, staring through the bobbing and weaving Marsh.

Bobby lunged in with a quick punch combination, but frowned as his ghost faced antagonist dodged each attempt, his head seeming to move independently from his neck. Bobby jumped up and down on the spot a few times then leapt up for a round house kick. What he glimpsed as he completed his mind air pirouette, made the hairs on the back of his neck stand on end. Ghost face's legs were planted, however his whole torso had bent backwards, leaving his body frozen at an impossible 90 degree angle.

Bobby's fists fell, as he stood, mouth gaping in disbelief. Ghost face stayed in this state, as if letting the reality of what the gangster was witnessing really sink in. When his upper body sprung upright, he seemed to simultaneously glide towards Bobby, who let out an involuntary shriek of fear.

And there the pale man stood, nose to nose with Bobby Marsh.

"W… what the hell are you?" Marsh whimpered.

PART 4 (DANNY ADAM'S APARTMENT)

"Ok so you're ere, you didn't give me much choice in the matta, and, let me get this right, you aint even tellin me what all this is about?" Danny Adams asked, in a distinctly put-out tone.

The introductions had been somewhat hasty, including first name and profession only.

Dax and Helen looked at each other. "I will mate, it's just not the right time," Dax said. Danny stood in the doorway to the living room of his two bedroom Finchley apartment, arms folded, glaring down at his two impromptu guests.

Dax and Helen sat round shouldered on the leather 3three seater that faced the room's focal point, a giant, wafer-thin television. The sound was muted. Danny sighed, dropped into his recliner and pick up the TV remote. "Alright, so I'm guessing this is work related then?" Danny probed. "Danny I can't, not yet," Dax reiterated. "Fine! So have I gained two overnight guests? Can I at least ask that?" "Oh no, nothing like that" Helen quickly confirmed.

They sat in silence for a few moments. Danny rolled his eyes and turned the TV up.

"3 innocent members of the public killed"

"Beginnings shrouded in mystery and conspiracy theory"

"10 Death-sentenced prisoner disappearances"

"Tens of millions in tax payer money spent"

"However, city crime is at its lowest since records began, plus breaking sources tell us that the notorious drug and people trafficking network "Wolf" has been shut down in the last 24 hours"

"So the question is simple...Was the government right to privatise London Met Police?"

"Good Evening and welcome to the Carter Report"

Helen frowned and shifted uncomfortably in her seat. Danny picked up on this

"What's up?"

"Oh nothing, I'm fine"

"Ah come on" Danny persevered "We gotta tawk about samink!" Danny scowled at Dax. "It's just; I am not that keen on Melvin Carter," Helen admitted.

"What, you serious? "Danny exclaimed. "MC's a legend, I love the way he gets piggy eyed politicians onto his show and then destroys 'em, it's hilarious! You can't tell me you don't enjoy that, didn't you say you was a journo?"

Clyne locked in. "That's exactly the issue, I'm a journalist, that's why I see through his lazy lead pilfering and one-sided documentaries."

Melvin Carter had been granted his own eponymously titled current affairs show, off the back of his political segment on the nation's most popular breakfast show "Rise".

He would spend this segment hounding what he called "questionable" government figures and "underperforming" members of parliament. His no nonsense, hard hitting style was an instant hit and it was inevitable that he would eventually be given his own hour-long primetime documentary / current affairs show.

Helen Clyne had seen this type before.

Although they usually started off with honourable intentions, that kind of reporter needed the drama, they fed on it, to the extent that it would become an obsession of sorts. However, front page scale scandals didn't occur every week, so the only way to sate the desire was to create one. Although even Helen would admit that Carter wasn't the worst of these types, his journalism was still very lopsided, and she felt he often went after the wrong person. This would usually end up with the vilification of bit part players. In the midst of all the noise, the spotlight would inevitably stay off the real villain, whom it would be trickier to expose.

She had also heard grumblings within her work circles about Carter's questionable methods when gaining leads.

"Oh come on, how can one journo criticise another for using shady tactics, are you telling me you aint never bent the rules even slightly in your fava?" "Danny come on mate," Dax pleaded. "No it's ok Andy." Helen was actually enjoying the respite of lighter conversation.

"I am not saying my history is whiter than white, but there's a line, a line which Carter consistently toes. I mean look at his report on the Archbishop a couple of years back."

Carter had blown the lid off a child molestation

epidemic within the Church of England two years ago, for which the then Archbishop took the majority of the heat.

"That guy was a filthy fackin paedo, he deserved everything he got!" Danny's tone oozed vitriol.

Helen sprung forward in her chair. "You see that's exactly my point. Let's look at the facts, he stood down voluntarily, and he himself was never charged with any crime. However, it was Carter's small minded journalism along with some slick editing that turned the notion you so eloquently put forward into common knowledge."

Although Dax was glad Helen and Danny had "hit it off", he was starting to feel a little spare, and was looking for a chance to politely ask Danny to give them a moment alone. After all, this was the point of going there in the first place.

Danny leaned forward and tipped his head as if mulling over Helen's theory.

"So you're sayin' he's innocent?"

"No, but he's guilty of ignorance and incompetence, not paedophilia. It's Carter and others like him who consistently manipulate the general public into eating what they're feeding them."

There was a pause. Dax snatched his window of opportunity. "Erm guys sorry to interrupt, but as I mentioned earlier, the reason why we came here is because Helen and I need to have a chat in private, and it's pretty urgent, so…" He stared at Danny. Danny stared back, frowning at first.

The look of realisation eventually spread across his face. "You're joking right?" Danny then turned to Helen, "Is he joking?" Helen grimaced and turned to face the TV, the uncomfortable silence continued.

"Are you really kickin' me aat my own livin' room?" Dax squirmed at hearing the reality of what he was asking of his best friend. "I know it's a bit rude mate, but I only need 10 minutes tops, I'll owe you one big time". "You'll me more than bloody one," grumbled Adams under his breath as he stormed out of the room. "Don't touch naffink!" Adams commanded behind him as he stomped across the passageway to his bedroom.

Dax looked up at Clyne, she grimaced in embarrassment. "Oh don't worry about him, he talks like the artful dodger but I consider him my mate!" It was Dax's turn to cringe in embarrassment at his poor quality joke. He lowered his voice and leaned in, "Seriously, he's a good bloke, I've known him most of my life". Helen frowned "Yes, but we pretty much forced our way into his house, then marginalised the area he could occupy within said house!"

"Believe me, we have an understanding, I've helped him out of some serious pickles in the past. Besides, it's just because he feels left out, I'll make something up tomorrow," Dax reassured.

2 PART 1 (BAXTER/ROBSON)

"**B**axter, have you lost your friggin' marbles?" hissed Head of Operations (formally Chief of Police) Walter Robson.

Walt Robson had hurried down to the large engineering workshop which constituted the Robotics Dept., scurrying down lane after lane of powered down Drones. He eventually found Felix Baxter in a patently unoriginal place, his office. "You sent those two on their first job unarmed, what the hell were you thinking? This was Wolf for god's sake!" The robot man shrugged. "All 5 targets were subdued, arrested and are now in secure holding, as planned," Baxter yawned flippantly.

"Yeah, 'subdued,'" Robson smirked sardonically. "And you think that that's the best way to spend tax payers' money do you, reconstructing the faces of soon to be executed criminals? Van Hassel's still touch and go, you know, he might not make it through the night!" F

elix Baxter grimaced as to feign embarrassment.

Walt Robson was getting sick of being undermined. He'd been reluctant to OK the use of Sark and Abercrombie for the Wolf pick up, and had thus far managed to successfully put off their general commissioning for the last couple of months. However, Cleaver was getting antsy. That, coupled with the fact that the drones were out of action until further notice had forced Robson's hand. However, the bare-faced arrogance of sending the previously untested pair into such a volatile environment completely unarmed, felt like a step too far.

"Walt, take a pill will you?" Baxter said quietly, "sometimes you have to take a calculated risk. Take a minute to think of the message this will send out. All five leading members of the most notoriously ruthless trafficking gang in Europe, assailed in less than 5 minutes, and that with Sark and Abercrombie at minimum capacity? How can you not be happy with that?"

"Happy." Robson pondered Baxter's unarguably intoxicating theory, and then shook his head vigorously as if snapping out of a spell. "You've cost us money, you've damaged our case, and you may have killed one of the most useful sources of info on Wolf's Europe-wide operations. So don't give me that shit about messages, this aint a bloody propaganda exercise!" "Isn't it?" Baxter smiled smugly. There was a pause, they stared at each other intently, like chess opponents. "Is the Doc aware of your little stunt?" Baxter stared at Robson and squinted. "I asked you a question," Robson probed. Baxter smirked again but said nothing. Robson leant in and lowered his voice.

"Look, you jumped up little grease monkey, you might think your shit don't stink just coz you can weld, but remember this, law enforcement is still my baby, and I say whether those two go out or not. So any more stupid moves like that, and I WILL be getting the doc involved."

Robson stormed out and slammed the door behind him, wobbling the door's window.

PART 8

ANDREW DAX (BLOG ENTRY)

I've met a girl…

But it's not like that.

Helen Clyne is a journalist, and by the little that I've already learnt of her, a bloody good one at that. She's not one of the sharks though; she's actually a geek journo. A geek journo who used to read a poxy little tech blog I ran about 3 / 4 years ago! Not just a geek journo, who used to read my poxy blog, but a geek journo who happens to be a complete Zeke Cleaver nut, and knows one or two very juicy secrets that only the Boss and his nearest and sneer-est are privy to.

We met a few days ago, in a boozer… wait, that's not really important.

What is important is the outcome of that meeting. She tragically lost her brother not long before we met. The cause of his death was said to be a massive electric shock, apparently generated from underground. Helen believes this unarguably freakish accident is somehow connected to Portentis Power.

For me, the inescapable fact is that a large part of England's capital is literally being powered by an alien. I admit this is a very crude analysis, but consider the evidence, Niroplaxia Gamonite is registered as a "living" organism, said living organism was not found on this planet. Now I am no law on the subject, but I was always under the impression that those two facts make the LC Element a textbook alien. There are many that feel that the two years spent on testing was nowhere near enough time to be sure that the organism was safe to install and begin sucking at its electrical teat. Ironically Helen wasn't one of the naysayers; in fact, I get the impression that up until the incident with her brother, in her book Cleaver could do no wrong.

Bottom line is I've agreed to print off some readings for her. Risky? Probably. Intrigued enough to risk it? Definitely!

Let me explain why, you see Helen Clyne has a quite unique source for her inside information. He goes by the name of The Bear, although I wouldn't have said he was christened as such.

Now I know of this guy, he's a hacker; well I've heard he's more like *the* hacker. The title "cyber safe cracker" has commonly been used when describing some of this web wizard's accomplishments.

Allow me to give you the tip of the iceberg.

In an earlier "self-blog", I mentioned a profoundly disturbing encounter I had with a member of CCC's security personnel. Remember the cold handed guy?

Well his hands were deathly cold because he was in fact, dead.

He is one of two criminals who were executed just under a year ago.

Before the plug was pulled, the doomed felon signed an agreement to take part in a new project being carried out by the CCC. This would have entailed effectively donating his body posthumous, in return for a very substantial pay out to an individual or party of his choosing, along with the chance of doing that one last "good thing". Although I'm not sure how many self-respecting hardened and condemned criminals would be sold on the latter.

Now the technicalities of what would have happened next would be lost on me, even if explained.

Suffice to say that the candidate would then have been kind of "hollowed out" and the resulting body/machine is then navigated by an officer at the Central Enforcement office, sort of like a "radio controlled corpse" (eloquent, isn't it?).

That cryptic ad campaign kind of makes sense now, as it seems that these two are prototypes for what is being planned as the successor to the CLED, branded as "Commissars". And here I was thinking the CLEDs were a creepy concept!

Typical isn't it, I was always optimistic that modern technology would eventually bring us the long anticipated and fabled "flying car" or "time machine", instead we get The Terminator!

For some twisted reason these two have retained their names posthumous.

Sark and Abercrombie. They sound like an interior design company to me. Anyway, maybe these two get to keep their names out of some kind of weird sentimentality, being the first prototypes and all, I'm not sure.

Helen didn't know their first names, but I'm hoping for something equally as festive. I don't know how many of these things are in "production", or when they will be officially unleashed on us en masse, but I am guessing, due to recent events, launch may be brought forward somewhat.

I know about this, because the Bear knows about this. The Bear knows more about the inner workings of the CCC than I could ever have imagined an outsider could know. Evidently he and Helen go back some way, and the Bear has promised to help Helen get to the bottom of what happened to her brother. In order to do this as efficiently as possible he needs a set of readings directly from the Portentis Engine. Now, the Bear has apparently never managed to bag any souvenirs from within the walls of the Sanhedrin, or indeed even been anywhere near to the place.

Think back to what he has already siphoned from hacking alone; now imagine the amount he could achieve if he actually got his mitts on something tangible, direct from the engine.

Why am I going out of my way to help someone I hardly know?

Well firstly, I had already decided it was time for a career change on the weekend of the Drone malfunctions; and learning of the Corp's gruesome and frankly morally outrageous plans for the future, well that's just served to confirm the clarity of my convictions.

Secondly, hearing Helen speak of her brother and the incident that resulted in her losing him, it really struck a chord with me. If I can help her get the answers she longs for by simply grabbing a few print outs from an establishment which I have already decided I no longer want to be associated with, well, why wouldn't I?

PART 9
ANDREW DAX (BLOG ENTRY)

London's becoming a strange little island.

Before Pulse/Drone-kill, the city centre didn't feel a world apart from Manchester or Birmingham. The main and most obvious sensory difference was that in London you'd hear the odd warm hum of a CLED unit as it would glide by whilst on routine patrol. That said, by all accounts this sound was gearing up to be commonplace everywhere within a decade or so, such was the adoration for these things. Well that is before "EXTERMINATE!" weekend, mind you.

The pulses are happening around twice daily now and they are preceded by electrical blackouts which last a couple of seconds each. It's actually making national news; they call the pulses "mini earthquakes."

The Sanhedrin, along with sporadic parts

of the city, are now suffering from this strange phenomenon, and people are getting spooked.

The fact that the South and Central London's police force has been severely decimated isn't helping the mood either, but that's a kind of fear that dares not speak its name.

For example, whilst waiting for my train into work a couple of days ago, something very strange happened. Picture the scene…

a crowded tube station, complete with the obligatory group silence, which has become synonymous with the capital.

It's a cool crisp morning. The people who haven't blocked the rest of us out with the use of fruit based music devices, have their noses securely lodged in newspapers or are poking away at tablet devices. There's a docile early morning calm.

I'm not too aware of those around me; I never am at this hour.

I'm just standing, staring at the graffiti on the tube wall opposite, and learning that "DA ILFORD MASSIVE A RUN TINGS!" The only person I notice is a middle-aged man to my right. He's short and painfully skinny with patchy, wispy brown hair desperately clinging to a bulbous cranium. His severe silver rimmed round-lensed spectacles along with a meticulously well kempt moustache make him look like an accountant from the 1950s.

A faint sound becomes apparent from

street level and grows in volume. Foot-steps, running footsteps.

These frantic and rapid footfalls seem to be swiftly approaching the entrance above us.

I look up towards the steep concrete steps at the far right of the stop, which lead directly to us. I wonder what or whom the feet are rushing to or from. The spectacled, pune-meister beside me flicks a glance up to meet with mine. He looks inexplicably nervous.

As the sound gets louder, laboured, panicked breaths provide accompaniment to the sprinting feet, along with the confirmation that the thundering footfalls have indeed begun descending the concrete stairs.

Those with unprotected ears begin to project the same sense of unease as the little moustached guy.

Gradually those with earphones in begin to notice the furrowed eyebrows around them; most eyes are now fixed on the steps, and are marked with a kind of weird agitated anticipation. Earphones are removed as the infection continues to spread.

As the footsteps get closer, a current of irrational panic begins to buzz through the group of commuters.

"What the hell is this?" I think to myself, as the virus begins to creep into my own system. The panting from above is now louder than the footsteps, and it becomes clear that the rationale behind this person's rush isn't in avoidance of missing a train. The volume of the wordless hysteria ratchets up a notch, and the group inexplicably begin to edge away from the mouth of the stairwell.

The desperado's shadow is now visible at the top of the final set of steps.

Fully grown, previously rational adults are now unashamedly cowering from the unknown sprinter, some are even feigning the sudden realisation that they are at the wrong stop and are walking away briskly.

I stand firm, determined not to submit to this rapidly spreading virus. As trainer-wearing feet become visible from the gloom at the top of the stairwell, something grabs my arm.

I gasp in surprise and look down from the steps to identify my assailant. The little accountant type is clinging to my arm!

I'm about to pull myself free when I notice that he too is staring intently up at the approaching feet, eyes bulging with fear. I realise that this is an involuntary action and that he isn't even aware that he's regressed back to childhood and is now desperately clinging to a parent.

Growing beneath the very essence of this man, is a previously dormant tumour of fear, now suddenly nourished by this fast approaching harbinger of uncharted danger.

The general psyche of a whole city summed up in less than 10 seconds.

I don't know why, but I don't tug free of the little man's needy grip.

Our harbinger's identification becomes apparent as he finishes his ascent.

He is a child.

A young Indian lad, I would say no older than fourteen, bolted toward us.

A person to my left lets out a strangled shriek.

As the boy approaches, I notice his eyes, glistening with fresh tears and trance-like with terror. Looking at this boy's horror-stricken face, it is obvious that his fear dwarfs any that may be smouldering within each one of this group of commuters. Everyone, including me, cowers back and holds their breath; however, the boy makes no eye contact with any of us as he tears past. He leaps down onto the tracks and disappears into the perfect blackness of the tunnel.

The crowd exhale as one, and the little guy lets go of my arm and offers an embarrassed grimace.

This experience has disturbed me more than I thought it would. Normal, rational people do not become paralysed with fear when they hear a person running. This occurrence is especially unremarkable around public transport. This unease could arguably be due to the aforementioned current lack of police protection in the city centre. I remember reading of a case, years ago, of a young electrician who sprinted down tube station steps, to his eventual doom, courtesy of the "old Met".

The thing that haunts me immeasurably more than this is the boy himself, his face frozen in a rictus of terror.

The only appointment that is guaranteed to be honoured down a London underground tunnel is by that of a high speed train.

Who or what could have conjured such a blind and frantic kamikaze flight instinct within this kid?

None of my fellow commuters seem to wonder or indeed care about the fate of the young lad however, but that's London for you I guess, every man for himself.

Following the "mission impossible" bit I'm doing for Helen Clyne, I have already decided to hand in my notice. But the weird tube station phenomenon has made me wonder whether that's enough.

Maybe I need to get out of London all together, go and become reacquainted with the rest of the country, with the *English.* There used to be a phrase banded around called the "London Mentality," this was a stick which was commonly used to beat all Londoners with. The privilege of using this particular stick was reserved for anyone residing north of the Watford Gap.

It would allude to an inherent selfishness projected by London folk along with a flippant dismissal of anything or anyone from outside of the M25 belt.

However, now more than ever I sense that the city is becoming more and more insular by the week. I have always thought (admittedly rather hypocritically considering that I'm on the payroll) that Cleaver Corp holds a disproportionate amount of cards when it comes to the general, strategic running of the City. Strangely though, it seems that only now have the English government snapped out of their stupor and noticed this slow and subtle estrangement with the rest of the country, as if it had been struck with a trance of lethargy by the low crime levels and the eerily sedate quiet that had fallen over the place during the last 20 years or so.

Yeah, you know the more I think about it, the idea of a change of scenery feels right. Escaping the ear popping, sweaty-pitted nightmare that the Sanhedrin has become is one thing, but escaping London itself feels somehow just as important, maybe more so.

I don't know why, maybe I'm starting to inhale the slow release paranoia which is spreading across the place.

My dreams are now filled with highly disturbing imagery. Giant Cybercorpses taking to the streets in search of a fresh harvest. Sometimes there are flashes of Rob Clyne being tossed around like a rag doll by some unseen underground behemoth. Man, chill out Andy!

I'm at risk of bringing on my own panic attack here.

Anyway, tomorrow is Friday and I'm doing a late shift. Just before I clock off at

9pm, it'll be a quick nip up to the computer room, grab a few choice print offs, get them home and then out on the beer with Danny Adams.

He has a knack of being able to lighten even my heaviest of moods.

5

"I'm still not sure how comfortable I am with the timing of it Ezekiel, it feels a little hasty, a little knee-jerk." The Prime Minister shifted uncomfortably in his seat.

The office towards the back of number 10 was smaller than Cleaver remembered. The PM had called Ezekiel Cleaver yesterday to summon him to an impromptu meeting upon hearing of the Doctor's desire to deploy the Commissars early. Cleaver liked the politician but didn't really respect him. Although he was personable enough and seemed to genuinely care, he lacked the required killer instinct it took to make those "un-makeable" decisions, and Cleaver felt this weakness would eventually be the ruin of him.

"I suggest a phased approach, you know, ease the public in. Just Sark and Abercrombie at first, bed them in." Cleaver lowered his voice slightly. "If we can build some trust in them, it would allow us to introduce another couple in maybe six months or so."

Cleaver's phone vibrated in his hand. The sound was faint, the PM hadn't heard it. He flipped it over to reveal the identity of the caller. It was Felix Baxter. "Why in god's name would he call me now, he knows I'm here!" Cleaver thought as he pushed END.

The PM leaned back, clasped his hands together and brought them up to his chin as he considered the Dr's proposal. "Well, public safety and law and order are my absolute priority here." Cleaver leant in, "mine also!" "I still think we could be utilising the armed forces, you know, to pick up the slack for the time being. It is peace time after all." Cleaver felt a sting of exasperation at this man's lack of backbone. "Can you really afford that? Deployment of the Commissars was diarised for six months from now anyway, is it really worth spending huge amounts of public money on a twelve month sticking plaster, when the answer is ready and available?"

Cleaver's phone buzzed again.

Baxter, what the hell? Again, he pushed END.

The head of government furrowed his eyebrows, "What's the CLED situation?" Before the professor could respond the PM continued, "Because if I'm to ok this I need to be confident when telling the public that what happened with those two drones was absolutely an isolated incident." The exasperation rose in the doctor again. "With all due respect Prime Minister, let me ask you this, the last time a member of the public died via human error on the Met's part, did you cease all operation and recruitment until you were sure that all possibility of human error had been eradicated?" "There's no need to be facetious Dr Cleaver!" The PM admonished. "Sir, I apologise if I appear that way but I don't mean to be (he did a little). Please believe me when I say that it troubles me gravely that my company's creation has caused any sort of harm to human life, I just don't believe it's fair that almost 20 years of immaculate functionality and service be forgotten in the malaise." The two men stared at each other in silence. Cleaver could feel he was close to the result he craved, so he thought he would give it one last nudge. "Look, I fully understand your concern, but Sark and Abercrombie are controlled entirely by Ops Officers at Central Enforcements; this drops the risk factor to almost zero" Silence.

"Ok Doctor, two commissars for a six month trial period. You step up the publicity campaign and I will make the announcement next week, then we can set a date for a month from then."

The doctor smiled, "thank you sir, I won't disappoint you."

Buzz…Cleaver glimpsed down at his phone, an email this time. He was able to navigate his way around the device without looking at it. He reengaged the politician's eye contact, whilst opening the email under the desk.

The PM smiled nervously, "Let's hope not, aye?" The phone on the PM's desk rang. "Please excuse me, Doctor," he said as he answered the call.

Cleaver smiled, nodded, and then subtly looked down again in order to glimpse the email.

 From: Baxter, Felix
Subject: Drone Malfunctions

Dr Cleaver, I am very sorry to bother you, I understand you are in an important meeting, but I need to speak with you urgently.

I have discovered the identity of the person responsible for the Drone malfunctions.

Please call me back at your earliest convenience.

Regards
  Felix Baxter
  Head of Robotics

Computer Cop Corporation
  Cleaver Corp

PART 10

ANDREW DAX

For the first half of the day, Andrew Dax had been floating around his office on a cloud of elation. This elation was fuelled by an overwhelming sense of relief.

After much back and forth, he had decided to resign from his post at Cleaver Corp. Even the fact that he didn't have alternative employment already secured didn't worry him. A man with his skill set wouldn't be unemployed for long, plus he had plenty of savings. Andrew Dax wasn't the only one who had decided to quit the Corp since the drone malfunctions a couple of months ago. Even with no knowledge of the company's macabre plans, the pulses, excessive heat and blackouts alone were undoubtedly issues which could have pushed some over the edge. The feeling of bubbling discontent had been exacerbated by the apparent lack of action to rectify the problems.

As the day had rolled on, the feeling of elation had been slowly superseded by a mild nervousness. Dax's working day had started at 12:00pm and he was due to be sipping a cold Friday night beer with Danny at approximately 9:45pm. The time was 8:43pm. The nervousness, he decided, was fuelled by the promise he had made to Helen Clyne a few days ago.

When Dax enters the main central lift at the end of his shift, he will be going up not down. His destination will be the Computer Room. His self-given assignment is the tricky task of smuggling a couple of Portentis' output readings out of the building. Dax knew that the hand-held scanners brandished by the meat heads at reception whilst state of the art, were unable to identify paper. Where the gamble lay was in the random manual searches carried out periodically by the aforementioned meat heads. However, the fact that footfall down at main reception was much slower at this time of night, made the gamble much less risky.

As Dax slowly rose he was relieved to be alone in the lift. He was usually grateful that the space came sans elevator music. Tonight though, the silence seemed thick and slightly restrictive. Tonight, the subtle, plink plonk of generic stock Muzak would have brought a welcome distraction. As each floor's button number lit up, Andrew Dax started to feel the all too familiar stream of anxiety begin to seep into his mind like toxic gas. "Bollocks, not now!" he thought to himself. He felt himself quickly approaching that fine line between creeping anxiety and full-blown panic, but he knew what to do.

The attacks often struck completely without warning or catalyst, but Dax's counsellor had taught him a range of breathing and counting exercises which had been working quite well. He continued these as he left the lift and didn't stop until he was showing his security pass to the wall scanner at the entrance to the computer room. By this time the attack had died down sufficiently enough for Dax to refocus on the task at hand.

Walking into the large air-conditioned room, he realised he was no longer alone.

Steve Macintosh was a programmer who worked over in Central Enforcements. He was a warm and personable northerner, who Dax had guessed was in his early forties. It was by no means unusual to find Steve hunched over one of the programming units at the front end of the computer room, nonetheless Dax's heart leapt in his chest at the sight of his colleague. He grimaced and inwardly chastised himself for being such a jumpy.

Whether it was the incessant whirring of the huge cooling fans or because he was in a trance-like state of concentration wasn't clear, but Steve didn't look up from his work station or indeed seem to even realise someone else had entered the space.

Dax stood staring blankly at the programmer for a moment, then realised it would look decidedly less suspicious to make his presence known with a greeting. The alternative would be Steve looking up to find a fellow geek staring down at him gormlessly.

"Alright Steve?" Dax blurted, a little louder than he had planned. Visibly startled, Steve Macintosh's head shot up, however when his eyes met Dax's, a warm smile almost simultaneously lit his face. "Ahh Mr Dax, how the devil?" Dax smiled back, masking his nerves "Well it's Friday and I finish in mere minutes, so I am pretty damn fine, and your good self?" Dax really just wanted to get away and get this thing done, but the man's likability was hypnotic. "Ah well, you know me, having to burn the midnight oil as usual," Steve said. "We lowly CE men have to do something to bump the old wages up!" Steve smirked cheekily. This was a running joke between the two men, regarding Steve Macintosh's adamant stance that Portentis Power's IT personnel were paid more than those at Central Enforcements.

Dax rolled his eyes "Mate, I keep telling you, if you ever saw a Portentis payslip you would gain a newly found appreciation for your role over with the plastic police!" Steve Macintosh dropped his head back down to his monitor, but his cheeky smirk endured "I believe you Mr Dax, thousands wouldn't."

Dax found his most convincing chuckle as he started towards the back of the room where the Portentis and Com Cop control units were situated.

As Dax sat at one of the stations, he was careful to position himself in a way that afforded him a clear view of the rest of the room; this was mainly in case Steve decided to approach him in order to continue the light-hearted argument.

He rubbed his hands together then pushed the standby button at the top left corner of the keyboard before him. As he navigated through two of the three separate security pages, entering two separate generic departmental passwords, he felt a pang of exhilaration, a smile lit his face. This was his Indiana Jones moment! It was then that the pathetic reality of this notion truly occurred to him, the fact that this was as close to action movie hero antics as his life was ever likely to get. His smile faded.

The third and final log in screen opened up, with the username and password boxes dead centre. His username was andrew.dax, as he began typing this, the auto complete simultaneously kicked in, finishing off both the username and the asterisked password.

Andrew Dax knew immediately that something was wrong.

PART 11

Andrew Dax had always been overly cautious when it came to IT security, and had always been very careful to disable auto complete whenever he had set up or had to change any log in details, both at work or indeed on any of his personal machines.

He froze and stared unblinking at his automatically completed name and could have sworn he could hear his heart pounding in his ears over the imposing drone of giant hard drives and cooling systems.

Multiple theories had already begun to flood Dax's mind as to what was happening.

If he pressed 'Enter' now and was allowed access to the Portentis Power and Com Cop portals, this would serve as confirmation that someone had overridden his person-alised log in details in order to gain access to his files, commands and general data. There were literally only a handful of people within this branch of Cleaver Corp with that kind of clearance, and that handful didn't include him.

He slowly brought his left index finger up and felt the coolness of the smooth black enter key against his finger tip. He held his breath and pushed the button.

With a soft beep, the Portentis Power and CCC portal page opened and the two options glowed before him. A wave of dizzying nausea washed over him as he tried to figure out his next move.

"This is bad… this is really, really bad!" Dax thought to himself, his mind racing from one theory to the next, who? When? Why? Though there was absolutely no doubt in his mind that the "why" wouldn't be anything wholesome! His hand seemed to move independently of his will, it took the mouse and slowly moved the cursor across the screen until it hovered over the CCC icon, it then tapped it and entered. Ordinarily he didn't have much reason to venture over to this side of the companies systems, but tonight it seemed his left hand had taken control of proceedings.

He entered into the configuration and command file; this stored every programme note and command sent to Com Cops since their commissioning. Pages and pages of staff names sprawled up and down the screen, Dax's heart continued to pound in his ears. After several seconds the pages finally finished initialising. Leaning in and squinting, he began scanning the alphabetical lists, desperately hoping this was to be a futile exercise.

Within mere moments his hopes were dashed.

One single entry, under his name. "What the hell?"

He hovered the cursor over the name and realised his hands were shaking. Taking his hand off the mouse he leant back in his seat to try and regain his composure by running through a shortened version of one of his breathing exercises.

Dax took one last look around him to make sure he

was still alone, then grabbed the mouse and clicked into the file before he lost his bottle.

This is what he saw:

A.Dax.0000.1a
    CLED Command iiop..///4321
    U0000.8*
    4173.7980.0890/99

A.Dax.0000.1b
    CLED Command iiop..///4321
    U0000.14*
    4178.6981.0890/63

Andrew Dax didn't need to see anymore.

He physically rocked back in his seat, as a mushroom cloud of dread exploded deep within his gut sending plumes of panic floating up his spine to the back of his neck, his vision blurred and all moisture instantly dried from his mouth.

He didn't fully understand what he was looking at, but he knew what it was instantly.

These were Com Cop commands.

He had never been inclined to or indeed ever been asked to attempt to set Com Cop commands. Apart from the fact that he had no idea how to do this, it wasn't part of his job so he didn't really need to know.

U0000.8* and **U0000.14***, these were Drone Unit numbers.

"Holy Shit, I'm being set up!" Dax whispered as the enormity of what he was witnessing started to sink in.

His brain again raced from one variable to the next:

"They can't possibly make this stick." Then it turned around and headed in the other direction: "Of course they can, this is Cleaver Corp, this is your word against fucking CLEAVER CORP!" then his mind flipped again "Who the hell is "they" anyway, and why me?"

If he failed in attempting to clear his name, what kind of punishment would he be looking at? Would it help if he had more friends over in Central Enforcements? The questions piled up and bottle necked in his mind.

However, one fact was clear, current and unquestionably more pressing than any other...

It was time to run.

PART 12

Dax was about to shut the machine down and flee the building, although he hadn't yet decided where his destination should be.

It suddenly struck him "Shit, the print outs!" It was now blindingly clear to him that he was sinking, but he had made a promise and he was determined to honour it by helping Helen on his way down. He took one last look at the command codes under his name as if in the futile hope that doing this might find him mistaken this time. He wasn't.

Dax then closed down the CCC system and entered his password for the more familiar Portentis Power operating system -no auto complete this time! Doing this took a couple of attempts as his hands were trembling severely. He quickly found the read outs for the date of Robert Clyne's untimely demise, hit print then ran to the peripheral he'd sent it to, all the time checking that he was still alone.

He snatched the printouts, folded them messily and shoved them deep into his jacket's inside pocket.

"What is happening to me, whose decision was it to make me the scapegoat, and why haven't they already come for me?" The only one of these questions he dared hazard a guess at was the last. He assumed a small group or even an individual had set the trap but hadn't expected him to discover it first.

For now though the time for pondering complexities had to be placed on hold. Dax didn't bother to log out of each screen he had opened, but instead held the power off button for the obligatory 3 seconds to override the regular power down process; it felt like an age!

As soon as the screen blacked out, Dax walked briskly back through the room in order to exit, briefly turning to his right to check if Steve Macintosh had continued his "midnight oil burning" elsewhere in the building, which he had, the work station was unmanned.

Dax was glad for this small mercy, as he knew he was now completely incapable of hiding the panic which was currently surging through him.

As he approached the secured exit door a sudden wave of anger washed over him at the betrayal dealt to him by the company he had served for more than five years. He was suddenly determined that it wouldn't end this way. He showed his pass to the scanner, walked through the automatic doors and turned right heading towards the main lift. As he looked up Andrew Dax stopped dead in his tracks and gasped with surprise.

No more than five yards away and facing him dead on, stood Matthew Abercrombie.

6

> Very small changes in the starting position of a chaotic system make a big difference after a while. This is why even large computers cannot tell the weather for more than a few days in the future. Even if the weather was perfectly measured, a small change or error will make the prediction completely wrong.
>
> Some systems (like weather) might appear random at first look, but these kinds of systems or patterns may not be. If you pay close enough attention to what is really going on, you might begin to notice the chaotic patterns...

PART 13

Kim and Claire have been together for four years and loved each other very much, however for the last six months or so the spark has been somewhat fading.

They aren't sure whether it's down to overfamiliarity or simply the drudgery of day to day routine, but they're determined to do something about it. One of Kim's colleagues (whose chemical makeup seems to be a little heavy on the testosterone) finds it baffling that a young lesbian couple could face this kind of mundane relationship challenge.

Kim isn't sure what he sees when he imagines a female same sex couple going about their everyday lives, but she's convinced she is happier in her ignorance.

The wine course was Claire's idea, she is being sent on the course as part of her work within the food industry and thought it might be fun to have her partner tag along. Besides as Claire's employer was footing the bill for her tuition fee, they would only have to pay once, plus they like wine and both were born with inquisitive minds.

The time is 9:52pm and the weather is unseasonably mild for an October evening.

They are en-route from their second lecture, being pleasantly surprised at the first at the amount of actual tasting that is allowed.

They are not model students however, in fact they've spent most of tonight's lecture giggling like unruly teenagers and taking the piss out of their cartoonish, camp lecturer. It wasn't until tonight that they had learnt that wine actually has legs.

They are on their way home having just got off the 205 bus and are making their way back to their Stepney two bedroom home.

It might be the fact that the bus was crowded and theirs is a popular stop which several passengers tend to exit, or just that they are still tipsily whispering and sniggering away in their own world, but it isn't until they turn to walk down Clarke Street that they realise they are being followed.

Clarke Street isn't the best lit street in the area, and it lies adjacent to a park which doubles as a well-known crack dealing point. Those two facts make this one of the last streets you want to turn down, only to realise you're being tailed by an "unfriendly".

Claire notices him first, from the corner of her eye. He's short, stocky and she would have guessed that he was mixed race (Caribbean and Caucasian). He is hovering behind them with way too much purpose to be just another bus passenger who simply happened to be going their way. Sensing they are, at best about to be mugged, Claire subtly dies the conversation down adequately enough for Kim to pick up on it. Claire gives a quick yet meaningful stare into her partner's eyes then flicks them behind, she tries to do this simultaneously, hoping their tail hasn't noticed. Recognition, then fear, sparks in Kim's eyes. Realising the sudden silence, they both shoot their eyes around frantically, hoping to see another person out and about…no joy.

Tonight, at this particular moment there are only three people out on Clarke Street. Sensing the silence is dragging, Kim blurts out something inane about the weather, Claire "hmm's" in agreement.

Both women's minds are fuzzy with fear. These kinds of things didn't happen around here anymore, and they are horribly ill prepared.

Claire's mum has always been vocal with her unease with the couple "walking the streets" at night. This has only intensified since the CLED'S had been decommissioned.

With stocky still in tow, they're about to pass the park which, for some reason is only closed and locked up sporadic nights out of a week. Both Kim and Claire have previously agreed that this is playing into the dealers' hands.

Both are now desperately hoping that tonight is a night that they will find a padlock secured to the rusted green gated opening, thus ensuring access denial. The unlit overgrown entrance to the small park is an ideal night-time space for either the clandestine or the macabre minded to operate.

A yawning gap in the discoloured wrought iron gates confirms another dashing of their hopes.

Stocky is breathing heavily.

The two women look at each other, making a non-verbal agreement to run for it.

Too late, they feel the inevitable scoop and shove sideways into the darkness of the park entrance. Kim lets out a gasp of panic, as she glimpses the large serrated hunting knife that their assailant is holding.

He corners them against the inside gate, the gloom cannot mask the malice in this man's ink black pupils.

He is brandishing the large knife in his right fist, bobbing back and forth in agitated fashion.

Both women are breathing quickly and shallowly, too scared to scream.

"Anbags, now!" he growls.

Kim clutches her bag close with one arm and her partner closer with the other "but we don't have any…"

"I don't bizzniz, gimme both bags now, don't make me peel off both yer heads, coz dat would get messy!"

A visible snarl turns his top lip up. "Filthy fucking dykes." The vitriol in his tone corrodes the night air.

He takes a step towards his captives, they both gasp in unison.

He freezes… his expression changes.

He drops the knife.

Both women simultaneously feel a sharp stabbing pain in their inner ears, then their world falls silent, all sound has been completed blotted out.

The fear and panic that had once engulfed the two women, is now evidently infecting their assailant. His eyes are bulging and his mouth is contorting in a grimace of agony, he clutches his stomach and begins to convulse.

Kim and Claire are silent screaming, their world still on mute.

They both now know that the man before them is no longer a threat, however the terror of an impending attack, is now being overridden by a cold blank vacuum of dread, sustained by confusion and disorientation. Although suffering sudden deafness, they are both aware of the distinct odour of overheating electricity.

Claire is frozen to the spot, and seems to have fallen into a sort of horror induced trance.

Torrents of thick blood begin to pump from the terrified man's mouth and nose. He stumbles backwards, then freezes to the spot, his feet fastened to the grassy ground.

His upper body spasms are becoming more violent, sending flecks of blood up and out towards the couple.

Kim grabs Claire by the shoulders as she squints away panicked tears and cries **"RUN CLAIRE, FUCKING RUN!!"**

Claire hears nothing, but doesn't need to, she snaps out of her stupor.

Both women begin sprinting for their lives.

Part 2 (History)

This day, 15 years ago is a very important anniversary for Ezekiel Cleaver and his brainchild, Cleaver Corp.

This is because it was on that day that his conglomerate knocked Mexxion (the oil giant) off its 2nd place perch in the league of highest market capped companies in the world, it was the day Cleaver Corp posted a market cap of £222.67bn.

Cleaver is especially proud of this moment, because his company's passage into the higher echelons of corporate enterprise was less than welcoming.

His legal ownership of the LC Element was contested fiercely, not only by the British military and other government arms, but also international envy and nervousness had made for common background noise to the Doctor's professional life since the very beginning.

Cleaver's determination to maintain full control of the priceless find was annoyingly legal and thus saw his reception into the syndicate of the commercial elite treated with a quiet mistrust and a chilly distance.

Cleaver thrived on this.

His league standing however came not solely from the electrical energy that Cleaver had managed to harness and sell to a large and still growing London customer base, but was instead largely thanks to the sales of his international smash the Computerized Law Enforcement Drone (these were produced under the Computer Cop Corporation trademark). The worldwide sales to law enforcement agencies alone were spreading like wild fire, regardless of the scepticism coming from other sectors.

It was new technology, fully tested and deemed safe, that actually worked well, why wouldn't it sell? The deal made with London Metropolitan Police two years previous was a very important component to the story, as this agreement arguably gave the product, and by extension Cleaver Corp, its credibility.

However, although a large chunk of the capital was unarguably benefiting from "Drone Patrol" (indirectly bringing general city crime levels to a record low) the rest of the country were very much more tentative about putting these machines to work.

This was the year that Cleaver Corp truly arrived, and it was armed with not only a physical and actualised version of a machine that had been prophesied by sci-fi novelists and visionaries for countless decades, but it also holstered a source of power that could one day keep this world afloat.

Cleaver's mantra was a simple one: "I want to make the world a safer and more efficient place".

Although Cleaver Corp had many other irons in the fire, with the Element and the Drones alone, he was already going some way to achieving this mission statement.

PART 14

Helen Clyne sat slumped in the corner of her three-seater, her index and middle fingers drumming on the cool, soft leather.

She'd come home early from work as she was finding it difficult to concentrate in her cubicle.

Usually the buzz of phones, the hum of voices and the rata-tat of thunderous keystrokes energised her, but not today somehow.

The deadline for the submittal of her piece, "Stalemate over the Morality Issues within Human Cryogenics" was drawing dangerously close. There had recently been reports of a successful revival of a previously dying person in a state of cryopreservation.

The lead, forwarded by her boss, was really more about investigation than that of reporting.

The editor in chief knew that Helen was the best investigative journalist he had, so he had no problem passing her the potentially huge story, much to the envy of her colleagues.

However, she couldn't focus on the story. Her mind swam in a pool of Cleaver Corp, along with her new acquaintance, Andrew Dax.

She was desperate to know whether the analyst had succeeded in his selfless mission to bring her what could turn out to be the answer to her most burning questions.

She'd liked Dax ever since reading his tech blog some time back, but this gesture that he had offered up, within mere hours of meeting her, went way beyond the call of duty. At first she felt a sting of suspicion at his quick willingness to put so much at stake, and so quickly. However, Helen Clyne knew without a shadow of doubt that she possessed an excellent judgement of character. There had been more than one occasion, professionally, that her very life had literally depended upon this gift.

Andrew Dax was a good guy, he was no hero mind, but he seemed genuinely intent on quitting Cleaver Corp and remained adamant that he wanted to help. Admittedly she guessed that this willingness was partly because he himself was intrigued by the whole thing. She recalled his expression upon learning the true identity of Sark and Abercrombie.

She picked up her mobile phone for the third time that evening, found the last call under the name A.D and hit CALL. The call rang out for a good ten seconds, then the answering service again informed her that Dax's phone was unavailable. Helen slouched back hard on the couch letting out an exasperated raspberry through her pursed lips.

"He must have received my missed calls earlier, what the hell's happening over there?" Then the unsettling thought emerged in her mind: "What if he's been caught…searched…arrested?"

She got up and grabbed the TV remote, turning on the set. The urgency in her movement was as if she was convinced the television would offer an immediate answer to her sudden concern.

Helen turned channels until she found the 24 hour news broadcast.

This was a world news offering, so she had to wait for the cycle to fall once again onto UK current affairs.

"Come on, come on," Helen pleaded, though she had no idea why.

Finally, the non-stop programme returned to UK news.

The very first news flash glowed before her.

It was London based.

Helen froze as she took in the pictures that were being accompanied by a voice-over from the correspondent at the scene.

She gasped... her mouth fell open...

She dropped the remote to the floor, breaking the device open, sending the batteries rolling across her living room floor.

7

A significant portion of Ezekiel Cleaver's business genius lay in timing.

The buzz around the Com Cop Unit was already reaching fever pitch when, upon the completion of two full years of testing and retesting, Portentis Power Ltd was officially registered and unveiled.

The company would boast an environmentally friendly and fully sustainable electrical energy service whose tariff charges ran at less than half of that of the cheapest in the area at the time.

Although Portentis Power had made big promises over its capacity to provide this new and exciting possibility to the whole of the capital and even beyond, London's main electricity supplier at the time was obviously very reluctant to relinquish any of its patch to the young, upstart company.

However, at this point the government stepped in, warning the aforementioned supplier of the dangers of "monopolising the market" and reminding them that the nation's leaders had a responsibility to provide its people with a sustainable, affordable and eco-friendly means of power. Portentis had unarguably proved that it could guarantee at least two of the three.

After months of being leant on by the Energy Secretary, the main supplier grudgingly handed over East London, along with a couple of districts that bordered Central London. This was under the obvious proviso that local interest to sign up was there in the first place…

A moot point.

Within two weeks of going live, 76% of private and commercial residents within Portentis Power's catchment area had signed up, withthe company's UK-based call centres ensuring smooth and prompt change over.

In fact, the company initially faced uproar from the rest of the city, then the rest of the country at the exclusivity of the coverage.

However the wheels are now very much in motion for national roll- out.

Hence the popular and current TV ad campaign that whispers "shhhh….Portentis is coming!"

Portentis Power now electrically power's 96% of East London and 85% of the Centre, with full city rollout due to be ready in less than six months.

Part 2 (Andrew Dax)

Andrew Dax stood momentarily transfixed. The Commissar Issue: 1 - labelled as **"MATTHEW"**, stood poised and ready to pounce not five yards from its target, staring into him.

The man-machine was standing between the analyst and the lift entrance.

"Shit… shit… shit!" was all that Dax could bring to mind at first. The reanimated law enforcer's eyes began quickly darting right to left. It seemed partially frozen, trance-like.

After a few seconds of nothing, Dax slowly leant forward, bringing a shaky right hand up and clicked his fingers. "Matthew" continued in its trance, eyes still darting back and forth as if hypnotized by a supercharged, invisible pendulum.

All the doubts that Dax harboured regarding his chances of out running this thing and getting away, had to be brushed aside. He knew it was now or never.

He threw a glance over his left shoulder, seeing the entrance to the stairwell exit that lay a couple of yards behind him.

In a fluid movement that belied his natural, physical abilities, Andrew Dax crouched, spun and exploded towards to the stairs.

Upon approach, he threw himself into the doors, he was surprised at first by his own agility, then by the absence of a cold hand grabbing and apprehending him. "Maybe I'm being paranoid. Surely if it wanted me, it wouldn't have waited politely outside for me to finish my errand? No, maybe it was doing something else. Maybe it wasn't looking "at" me, so much as "through" me." Even though this theory seemed immediately feasible, he didn't bother looking back to check on the delay in his apprehension, but instead used this leeway to steady himself and grab the stair rail, as he began hurtling down the first set of laminate covered concrete steps.

First set clear… heart pounding, mouth drying… second set clear, hissing panicked breaths through pursed lips…

Whip! Crack! The door he had plunged through seconds ago, imploded above him.

Destroyed along with the door, was the theory that Dax had no reason to run.

"Shit… shit… shit!" Dax's panic-induced Tourette's continued. "Well I don't think I'll need to hand in my notice now!" The sardonic musing flashed through his mind.

As he cleared the eighth set of steps, he guessed he had at least another 10-15 flights to clear before he reached Reception, the thunderous footfalls above him were now deafeningly close. Even if by some miracle, he did reach Reception, what then?

Dax came to the grudging realisation that this simply wasn't going to work.

He continued his ascent however, what else could he do?

He guessed the thing above him couldn't be reasoned with, so his desperate logic told him to continue as far as he could before his inevitable capture. He recalled those American "Most Deadly Police Chase" type programmes that came on late at night, and imagined that this must be how those desperados feel as the squad cars close in, and the their petrol-low light pings on. Not so much if as when.

He glanced behind him and saw "Matthew's" ominous shadow as it finished the flight of stairs just before his, "this is it" he thought.

Dax felt the presence of his relentless pursuer behind him, the cold hand was imminent.

He closed his eyes.

Then came an intense sound: a high pitched whistle which radiated into Dax's brain and threatened to burst his eardrums, he cried out and fell forwards. However he didn't meet the steps below him, face first, as physics would suggest.

In fact, his body rose flipped on its side...the whistling stopped... the world froze... **BOOOOOM!**

Dax felt himself being flung through the air, a crushing blow to his back...

Then Andrew Dax was outside.

PART 15

One area that Computer Cop Corporation is frequently criticized, is the presumed lack of impact the company has made on black street crime in and around South London. However, the cold numbers don't back this notion up.

In reality, the level of crime in general has lowered gradually, year on year in this area, since the CCC was established. The issue of *black crime* in this area has been well publicised down the years. With Ezekiel Cleaver at the very top of the chain of command for London's policing. This issue is raised and put forward to him with, what Cleaver has called "suspicious regularity". As if he was the *elephant in room* of sorts. He has often wished that the media would show a little more bravery and just come out and ask "being black yourself, don't you think you should be doing more?"

The reality was that, Ezekiel Cleaver had never been too interested in the issue of race.

This might be partly down to being preoccupied by the weight of tragedy that he'd been yoked with, and at such an early age. Cleaver would suggest that it simply isn't a subject that features frequently in his thinking. Some find this hard to grasp, being that he himself was part of a racial minority.

Being of Black Caribbean ethnic origin was something that the Physicist looked upon with simple indifference. "We are all but flesh and blood are we not?"

The 1980's fine artist Jean Michel Basquiat once declared "I am not a black artist, I am an artist." This is as close a representation of Cleaver's view as you can get.

Some circles believe his dismissal of such a provocative issue, is down to the fact that he is an intellectual, and possibly sees racism as simply another one of our species' more volatile or unseemly traits, like deceit or projectile vomiting.

In fact Cleaver finds it baffling that these debates about him happen at all.

Nonetheless, let us be clear on this, he doesn't devalue the issue as a whole. It's not denial or extreme apathy (for example denying the Holocaust ever happened), he just hasn't ever really related these issues directly to himself. Those that say that this is because he had a privileged and sheltered upbringing, are wrong and furthermore know nothing of his past.

Some sections have reacted indignantly at the scientist's seemingly flippant stance on such a worldwide subject. This moral displeasure is made even more inexplicable by the fact that most of this section have never met or indeed even taken the time to research the man's life and work from even a surface level.

One can imagine that Cleaver's belligerent side might kick in at this point and ask "so by your informed hypothesis, the reason that I am expected to carry some kind of responsibility for a whole race, is based purely upon the credential of belonging to said race?"

PART 16

News Report

"There has been a suspected explosion at London's Police headquarters."

"The combined CCC, Portentis Power and Central Enforcements building, the "Sanhedrin" has suffered an inexplicable building collapse, which has caused extensive damage to the west wing and front sections of the complex. Fire services are currently at the scene, but it is not yet known the extent of human casualties that this incident has claimed."

"However, it has been confirmed that Central Enforcement's holding cells at the back of the complex have not been affected"

Cut to pictures from the scene.

"This incident comes less than 3 months

after the full decommissioning of the Com Cop Support Units. This was due to the malfunctions that led to three tragedies in different parts of the capital. "This new development will undoubtedly raise fresh questions regarding Cleaver Corp's capability to continue its control of London's law enforcement provision."

Helen Clyne stood in her living room staring at her TV, mouth gaping in disbelief. "Snap out of it Clyne!" She ordered herself. She shook her head vigorously to clear her head; it worked, in a fashion.

She gathered up the broken remote and replaced the batteries. Retaking her position on the couch, she turned the volume way up and sat leaning forward, listening intently.

The rest of the report taught her nothing of the whereabouts or condition of her new friend.

Helen decided that in this instance, action was the best course of reaction. She turned off the television, shrugged on her jacket, grabbed her car's key fob and handbag then hurried out of her flat.

Part 5 (A new arm of Law Enforcement)

"Commissar" is the project coding for Computer Cop Corp's newest product.

The process is as follows. Death sentenced criminals can opt-in to the project, and in doing so are rewarded with a handsome financial package. Obviously the condemned individual must nominate the party that they would like to benefit from the pay-out (this is why the offering is most attractive to inmates with families). Within 24 hours of termination, the deceased is then put through the process of "Reanimation". This involves the careful skinning and gutting of the corpse, the brain is also removed at this time.

The redundant vital organs are then replaced with a state of the art hard drive and a large circuitry system unit.

The skeleton is then clad (reinforced) with a tough metal plating which uses the same mix of Titanium and Tungsten alloys as is used for the casing to the Portentis Engine. The joints and spine are supported with a mixture of pneumatic and hydraulic mechanisms. These intricate 360 degree moving components allow the re-animated body to move in dimensions that would have been impossible for a living, breathing human being.

The eyeballs are removed and electronic lenses are attached to the backs, the eyes are then re-secured. The empty cranium is fitted with a GPS tracking device, a cooling system, a small back up motor along with a range of tiny 3D /HD cameras.

The skin is then treated with a preserving balm and reintroduced to the reinforced skeletal structure. The relevant programmes are then downloaded to the machines hard drive. The machine is then synced with a control pod based within Central Enforcements, which allows the reanimated machine to be controlled remotely. Chosen Operations Officers are specially trained in the control of the unit. There are currently five single-person control pods at Central Enforcements, one of which has been set aside for training purposes.

Each unit is issued with two modified Desert Eagle .50 pistols. Only Commissars, Com Cops and authorised police personnel are ever issued with firearms.

Once they are powered up and under the control of an Ops Officer they officially become a "Commissar".

The Commissar is set to be a real game changer in automated law enforcement. The new unit is not only much faster, mobile and fluid in movement than the Com Cop, but the production, although much more complex and intricate is more cost effective than the Drone. The highly elaborate hand to hand combat and "Ultra Aim" fire arm programmes make the Commissar an adversary that is not to be underestimated.

Jason Sark and Matthew Abercrombie were the first two inmates to opt-in to the project.

8

I t was the dust and debris hitting the back of Andrew Dax's throat that had thrust him suddenly back into consciousness.

He gagged and coughed, raggedly jerking his body up to a sitting position, he was then quickly reminded of the blunt impact he had received to his back, and he winced. However, the pain in the centre of his back was a moderate ache as opposed to crippling agony. He squinted through the dust but couldn't make anything out just yet.

He rubbed his head as his hazy mind began to clear. "Has the building been bombed?" he wondered. The last thing he remembered was being pursued by the zombie cop, then being flung through the air. The fog that impaired his thinking, although lifting, was still quite thick. He started to notice the eerie quiet that encircled him. No sirens, screams, or residual explosions were apparent as yet.

Dax was relieved to find that he was able to get to his feet with relative ease. His vision had cleared somewhat too, however his throat still burned furiously, he coughed again and tried to muster some saliva to sooth his ragged oesophagus, with limited success. Although he didn't see

"Matthew" upon his first scan around, he knew he only had mere seconds to decide his next move, this was definitely the calm after the storm before the hurricane! He padded himself down in disbelief that he wasn't more severely injured, then he insured that the print out was still buried in his jacket's inside pocket.

A sudden vibration down his left leg made him cry out in surprise. He realised it was his mobile phone. Dax took a shaky hand and removed the handset from his trouser pocket. The screen was slightly damaged, but he was able to make out Helen's name.

He knew exactly why she was calling him. He hit END.

Then a scream to his left…

Running footsteps to his right…

Controlled, shouted commands emerging from the huge yawning hole in the complex in front of him.

"Time to go!" Dax thought as he fled down Stafford Street into the night.

PART 17

"Phipps! Where the bloody hell is Phipps?" Walt Robson boomed, speaking to everyone and no-one as he stormed across the work space towards the control pods.

Central Enforcements was a hive of frenetic energy and activity. The collapse at the other end of the complex shook the space that housed the Head of Operations and his team. Kai Phipps was the Operations Officer delegated to control Matthew Abercrombie that night. Phipps was one of only two Ops men trained to control that particular Commissar. 10 minutes ago, Walt Robson – Formerly Chief of Police – now Head of Operations had had to think and act far quicker than he had done for several years...like a copper.

Although the awesome sound had initially filled the former policeman with dread, the corresponding reaction which consisted of taking the first call from reception, explaining what had happened, then gathering and deploying his team along with alerting the fire department, had filled Robson with an invigoration that he couldn't help but enjoy.

"Its failed Chief, the machine's failed!" The zeal in Cartwright's words was unbridled. Tom Cartwright followed in behind Robson as the Ops Head searched out the Commissar's controller.

In the weeks that had followed the Wolf take-down operation, the professional identity crisis that Tom Cartwright had already been suffering from had understandably worsened. He was now hopeful that the Data Analyst's escape would sway his boss into sending human enforcers to at least make the relatively easy pick up. Robson heard the young officer but didn't acknowledge him. However Tom Cartwright was determined to get his point across and pursued his boss diligently.

"Me and Jarvis can go and pick up the Analyst, no bother whatsoever." Robson stopped and turned, looking exasperated. The Ops Officer lowered his voice "Please Chief we're gathering dust in here, we all are. This would be a piece of piss, we could bag him and have him back here in no time! You know I'm trying to stay busy, especially at the moment." Robson leant in towards Cartwright and spoke quietly, "I feel for you Tommy, I know how tough things are for you outside of work right now, I really do, but have you not noticed what has just happened here. Don't you think there's something more constructive you could be doing right now?" Cartwright opened his mouth to speak, but Robson continued "Look Tommy, Phipps was assigned to use Abercrombie to arrest the lad. Now I admit, that hasn't happened, but you can't say there hasn't been one giant extenuating bloody circumstance, now can you?!" "But Chief!" Cartwright started again, only to get cut off once more. "Now you listen to me, I didn't send you to scene of this building collapse or whatever the hell it is, coz you're not an ant," Cartwright frowned, Robson lowered his voice further and clarified "you're not Team Man, nor should you be wasting your time trying to score points off a friggin' machine!

I've always thought it, and your work on the Wolf case confirmed it, you're a Detective, son." Then Robson's face hardened again and he grabbed Cartwright by his scruff "Now stop wasting my time and start acting like a fucking Detective!" Robson was shouting now. "Come to think of it, I am gonna give you your first assignment…

FIND KAI FUCKING PHIPPS!!"

Part 3 (Ezekiel Cleaver)

Ezekiel Cleaver cut a lonely figure, sitting hunched forward on one of the leather recliners in the lounge area of his super-mid private jet.

The craft was hurtling back from Paris, Cleaver was wearily returning from one of his seemingly endless fire-fighting missions. He was determined not to let the Drone incidents make an unrepairable dent in sales.

Although he wasn't the kind of billionaire that travelled with an entourage, Cleaver would usually be flanked by at least two of his close men. Tonight though, he was one of only five men on board the light aircraft, and neither his two pilots nor two members of his security personnel were in the vicinity. He needed all of his British close men to stay in and around London on this one, way too much going on there! The Doctor was mulling over his latest monumental and pivotal career decision. "Andrew Dax is no one, we can surely do this neatly and without too much incident," Cleaver comforted himself.

Over the last couple of decades, the scenery of law and order within the English judicial system as a whole had changed extensively. Cleaver hoped this would help in his bid to be granted the behind-closed-doors trial and sentencing for Andrew Dax, under the Public-Interest Immunity act.

In rare cases, an order that PII applies to would usually be sought by the British government to protect official secrets, and so can be perceived as a gagging order. Where a minister believes that PII applies, he signs a PII certificate, which then allows the court to make the final decision on whether the balance of public interest was in favour of disclosure or not. Generally, a court will allow a claim of PII without inspecting the documents: only where there is some doubt will the court inspect the documents to decide whether PII applies.

This would tie in nicely with the brand new "Automated Manslaughter, By Proxy" and "Automated Murder, By Proxy" acts. Now these particular statutes had only just been passed by Parliament, due to the relatively new culture of "remote control law enforcement". Although similar new laws were being mulled over, the nation's law makers had been slow to respond to the changes in modern technology and their impact on society. It wasn't the first time this problem had occurred. The judicial system was equally sluggish to react to the advent and eventual all conquering revolution of the World Wide Web. Cleaver's plan for Andrew Dax was quite simple in principle. A quick and quiet trial and conviction for the Analyst, and a nice neat 7 – 10 year sentence under the new Automated Manslaughter, By Proxy act.

If successful, this would not only help to build a strong case for the re-commissioning of his Drones, but it would also give the Doctor breathing space in order to address more pressing issues.

The first of which was the damage to the Sanhedrin which had just been called in. The strange structural collapse had apparently not generated any fatalities. Cleaver hoped this was to prove correct as it would make it much easier to keep the media at arm's length with whatever explanation PR decided to feed them. Any problems with the Element or the Engine could and would be ironed out, outside the range of prying eyes.

The second was the task of holding together the fragile, depleted infrastructure of London's law and order provision. Random crime and antisocial behaviour had already begun to creep up over the last couple of months, and Cleaver was absolutely determined not to lose control of his city. Now he had the backing of the PM, he could confidently rush more Commissars into production. "I hope those Inmate Agreements have increased," he thought to himself.

There was another worry festering in the deeper recesses of his mind, however. Helen Clyne. *I know she knew about the Commissars, and I know she knows the analyst, but are these two facts linked?* There were things about the journalist that he needed to know, however he had to be very careful. Cleaver had bent ethical rules on more than one occasion during his business life, but owning the capital city's police force was completely different to any of his previous business ventures. Helen Clyne, was by all accounts a much-respected figure within serious journalism, plus she wasn't guilty of any offence at this point. Going in too ham-fisted would not only be teetering on illegal, but could end up more of a PR disaster than he was already facing. There might not be much recovery from the damage she could do, from that stand point.

Indeed this would have to be a carefully played game of chess with the reporter, depending on how well she knew the Analyst, Cleaver guessed there would be questions around his detention, and the prohibition of visitors. The family and less informed friends would be easier to sate. They know he works for the "Government", so something vague like... "Mr Dax is under investigation in a highly sensitive case, any form of communication is strictly prohibited at this stage. Further guidance will follow."

However, Cleaver knew this wouldn't wash with the journalist.

Part 4 (Helen Clyne)

A hazy mist of drizzle had already begun to coat Helen Clyne's face and hair by the time she'd unlocked her car and quickly ducked into the vehicle, slamming the door behind her. She shrugged and wiped her face, and with a groan of moist discomfort, leaned over and pulled her seat belt on.

She looked down at the gloom of the passenger side foot well, where she had tossed her handbag upon entry. Crouching down, she rummaged around for her phone, pulled it out and set in down on the passenger seat beside her, checking again in vain for missed calls.

She quietly but clearly recited her car's security start code thus turning on the ignition. She then asked for dipped head lights and intermediate wipers before pulling away.

Helen, again spoke clearly and precisely as she commanded her radio on, and then ordered the station she wished to receive. As she turned right out of her estate, the local news feed confirmed that the incident at the Sanhedrin complex was indeed a building collapse and not an explosion as first believed.

It also informed her that reports coming out of the scene were that all staff had been accounted for. Meaning, although the fire and rescue services were still hard at work at the scene, the only fatalities they believed they would find, if any, would be from any unfortunate passers-by at the time. "Andy, where the hell are you?"

The fact that Dax was most probably alive, filled her

with relief for his physical safety, but didn't help her confirm what had become of him. "He finished at 9:00pm right? I don't think the collapse took place till at least 9:45pm. Maybe he was already out." The comforting thought was quickly subdued by the fact that it was now 10:16pm and he hadn't called or indeed answered his phone. These thoughts and counter thoughts continued to ebb and flow in her mind as she took the exit for Stratford.

Then her mind switched to matters closer to home. Her last supper with Rob glowed warmly in her mind. Then an early memory emerged.

Even at the tender age of 9 Helen craved responsibility. She'd learned to ride a bike before Robert, their father (a somewhat strict and stoic character in their lives) decided that under his supervision, she could do the honours of teaching six-year-old Robert the basics. The joke was that after just a week under Helen's training regimen, the young boy had ended up in tears, begging to be schooled by their father. Robert never let Helen forget this, and even as an adult would sometimes feign fits of tears and call for his daddy, when she got too "naggy."

An icy gale of grief threatened to engulf her, as it had done at least twice a week since the night he passed. However tonight wasn't the night for this. She cleared her throat loudly, squeezed her eyes shut for a second and shook her head vigorously. Then ordered herself to keep it together, as she closed in on the Sanhedrin.

Fortunately, Helen was able to find a parking space midway down Stratford Street, around 75 yards from the Sanhedrin. From this vantage point she was able to make out the mess of blue flashing lights which were acting as a cordon for the front of the complex, but wouldn't be noticed vice versa. Perfect.

As she waited for the vehicle to parallel park, her phone vibrated beside her, Helen's heart leapt in her chest.

The smooth device nearly squirmed through her fingers and ended up under the seat, such was the ferocity of her movement. It was a mailer from Dax!

A rash of goosebumps flared up the back of her neck and continued into her scalp, her quickened heartbeat slammed against the underside of her ribcage. Helen took a deep breath, steadied herself and opened the mailer.

9

The Bear knows...

He sits in a dimly lit room, the warm glow of three separated computer monitors providing the only light, and they illuminate the hacker's pale withered face.

Streams and streams of code percolate frantically before him. He begins to cough violently, head bobbing, clutching his chest as he winces in agony between fits. He groans and with a shaky right hand grabs for the bottle of tablets behind the monitor directly before him. He guzzles two large blue pills, with a swig from the mug of cold black coffee on the far left of the desk.

The Bear knows why Units 8 and 14 malfunctioned...

His fingers thunder away furiously at two separate keyboards, one for each hand. Beethoven's Moonlight Sonata fills the small space, the mournful piano piece throbs around him from an elaborate surround sound system.

The Bear knows the intricate workings of the Computerized Law Enforcement Drone...

He is right now filtering classified code from the United Nation's network vaults, directly to his machine. He doesn't plan on using this sensitive data mind. No, this is exercise, he likes to stay sharp.

The Bear knows Ezekiel Cleaver's business plans for the next five years...

He is glad that Helen Clyne has gained a link inside The Corp who has agreed to help her obtain the print out codes that she so desperately seeks. He will indeed confirm for her whether her brother's death was caused by Portentis Power. However, he has a much more clandestine and personal reason for needing this information.

The Bear knows Andrew Dax, but Andrew Dax doesn't know him...

He smirks to himself coyly, revealing a mess of stained misshapen teeth. The prospect of collaborating with this young analyst fills him with a nervous anticipation. Helen had never met him face to face, nor had they ever had a verbal conversation. In fact the Bear hadn't had a face to face conversation with another human being in more than 14 years. However he knew he could not succeed in this mission alone. If this analyst is as good as Clyne says he is, he could be the perfect candidate to end the lonely hacker's self-imposed solitary confinement.

The Bear knows exactly how to get what The Bear needs...

PART 18

Sent by: AD

Helen

Something bads happened, no time to explain, apart from to say that Im not harmed.

Printouts r hidden in the ridge under the lid of a waste bin. It's the 1 situated at the malwood rd corner of st pauls park. Early in the morning is the best time to get it, no one about. One more thing, you're not in any immediate danger but for my sake do me a big favour and completely destroy the phone carrying this msg asap, please! I know its all very cryptic but the less you know the better at this stage, hope to c u again someday so I can explain things, but for now please don't attempt to contact me.

Gotta go away now and lay low for the foreseeable.

Was good to meet you and hope you find what u r looking for.

PS if I ever see you again I will pay you back for the phone!

Andrew

XX

Helen frowned at the message before her, and then read it again. She sat back in her seat and exhaled deeply.

"What the hell is going on?" Helen decided quickly that approaching the building just yards from where she sat, was now not only pointless, but by the tone of Dax's message, the action would do them both more harm than good.

She pulled out of the space and drove away.

Part 3 (Andrew Dax)

Dax was thankful that he had donned his hooded jacket this morning as the gentle evening drizzle of earlier had now become moderate rain.

The garment also aided him in keeping his identity shrouded. He stood hooded and hunch-shouldered along with two other strangers, waiting for next bus to Canning Town. They didn't give him a second look. His slightly crouching stance was partly due to his back, which still throbbed miserably. The impact with the collapsing wall was beginning to tell and not just on his back, he also felt an injury to his left thigh. The hood also hid a moderate gash on the back of his head. Upon revisiting the incident in his mind, he decided that apart from the collision with the crumbling wall, his limp, unconscious body must have fell at least a couple stories to the pavement outside. With this in mind, he couldn't help but admit that it was nothing short of a miracle that he hadn't suffered more extensive injuries.

This particular bus stop stood two streets from St Paul's Park. He now began to doubt the wisdom behind leaving the print outs in such a public place, however his options were greatly limited at this stage. If he was indeed now a fugitive, there was no way he could risk meeting up with the journalist.

He wracked his brain for his next move. "Can't go home, can't go to my folks." Then it hit him. "Oh god, my folks!" He realised that tomorrow morning he would be getting the weekly phone call from his mother. She always called him annoyingly early on a Saturday morning, as if she was trying to catch him out. Mother Dax was convinced that he partook of what she called the "wild city life" although nothing could be further from the truth.

She worried about him constantly, and at least once during the weekly conversation would urge him to return to Hertfordshire, where he had grown up, and where she and his father still resided. "What's wrong with a nice commute? Lots of people do it!" would be one of her favourite lines of reasoning. He couldn't help but crack a warm but melancholic smile. "God I love that woman."

He decided the best course of action in this case would be to cancel out the need for the call by phoning her tonight, as he had no idea where he would be by tomorrow morning.

More pressing issues began to crowd his mind. Like, where would he stay tonight? The only reason he was taking the bus to Canning Town was force of habit, as he would usually get the tube home from there. However, at this point he had no clue which direction he would head in tonight.

One of the strangers blurted out a strong profanity in response to a heavier flurry of rain.

Raindrops drummed down on his hood, making it wilt almost to the point of restricting his vision. He shook his head slightly, getting rid of the excess water.

Where to begin in the process of attempting to uncover the sabotage he had fallen victim to? He suddenly felt as small as an ant, an ant that Cleaver Corp had decided was small and inconsequential enough to squash, in order to solve their "little problem." Whoever had set this up on the company machines must have had considerable skill. It became apparent to him that he would need to call on the services of someone with matching or greater program-ming/hacking expertise, if he was to muster any kind of counter attack.

The bus arrived and came to a crawling stop. He let the two strangers get on first, as he was the last to arrive at the stop. Neither thanked him, this would usually have annoyed Dax, but tonight he was glad to be dismissed. He stared out of the window through the mist of steam and condensation as the bus lurched from street to street. He began to question whether it was even worth running and revisited his panicked thoughts of an hour ago as he hurtled down the Sanhedrin steps. "This isn't going to work." This time there would be no inexplicable yet timely "building-fail" to save him. With that thought, he looked down at his trousers, suddenly worried that they would still be caked in dust, however the rain had taken care of that problem.

These add-on thoughts were acting as distractions, the bus was creeping closer and closer to his stop and he still hadn't decided what to do when he got off. He frowned determinedly and took control of his thinking. "I need to get out of London" Done, there was no going back on that decision. "I'll give Alex or Jeff a call (old college friends), they both live in the Midlands and last time I spoke to either of them they didn't have families. I will ask to crash with one of them. Yes that's it, I'll say I'm there for work, and thought a visit was way overdue!" Done. That was the plan for the next 24 / 48 hours sorted at least.

He looked at his watch 10:34, a little late to randomly call either of his old buddies. He would make the journey north by train tonight, and stay in a bed and breakfast. Dax had been paid today, which was another small mercy. He decided to warily stop off at home first and gather some things, then begin his late night trip. He was hoping he could achieve all this whilst decoyed by the incident at the CCC.

Dax pushed the buzzer to make the driver aware that his stop was next, he thanked the driver as he stepped of the bus "what a polite, young fugitive you are!" he complimented himself. As he approached Canning Town underground the atmosphere seemed to thicken, the rain unable to disturb the city smog. He pulled up his hood and took out his phone, flicking through his contacts to find his parent's land line number.

"Hi Mum," he tried to sound as light and airy as possible. "What's wrong?" she asked worriedly. "Why would something be wrong?" Dax frowned and smirked. "Well, the time, it's late" her voice still quiet with concern. "I know but I'm living the crazy London life, remember? The party never stops round these parts!" Dax ventured playfully. "Very funny. What's up son? I'm on my way to bed. You're father's already snoring the house down!"

He went on to tell her that he was taking an impromptu trip to Spain for a week with some friends, but it had slipped his mind until then to inform her, so thought he would drop a call in now out of courtesy, as he knew she worried about him. This was met with grudging appreciation. "As long as you're around at Christmas, I know you know better than to disappear at Christmas!" "Yes mother" he replied dryly, doing his best to keep his tone as characteristically playful as possible. "Don't call me that, it makes me sound old!" "You are old" Dax teased. "Oi cheeky, you're going the right way to get hung up on!" She admonished.

The rest of the exchange remained light in tone, however it was the softly spoken words, "I love you son, goodnight and God bless," which brought their brief conversation to a close that had threaten to break Dax's façade of joviality. His heart swelled in his chest to the extent that it began to ache, his eyes burned with hot tears. "Goodnight mum, love you too, and give my love to dad." As he hung up, he realised that that could possibly be the last time he would hear that sweet voice as a free man for a long, long time.

His train home wasn't packed, but it was busier than Dax had hoped it would be. He picked up a free newspaper on his way to the quietest cab possible. He settled in his seat, and flipped through the press publication. It was too early for it to carry any news of the incident at Cleaver Corp HQ which had created the diversion aiding his escape; nonetheless, it did hold a story regarding some of the "Corp's" latest international exploits around chemical and cellular research. You could pick up any London based newspaper on any given day and be 99% sure it would make room for something Cleaver Corp based, being the jewel in the city's crown and all that! People entered and departed the cab that Dax occupied, however he was momentarily unaware of his surroundings, being unexpectedly engrossed in the article.

It was the sense of a presence directly over him that rushed him back to the moment. It was only then that he noticed how quiet the cab had become. He nervously began to hope that this was because the area had emptied considerably. But why would a person feel the need to stand so close to him in an empty cab?

He froze, eyes staring at the paper. The presence remained.

"Shit!" He whispered. Head still bowed, he took a glance to his right. What he saw confirmed his fear. Two women looking on nervously but not at Dax, instead they stared fearfully at the presence before him. He slowly raised his head up from the paper...

There his eyes met with Matthew Abercrombie's.

The humanoid's pallid lifeless face bore down on him oppressively; black, hollow eyes stared through him.

Dax's heart sank to pit of his gut.

Panic was pointless, escape?

Impossible.

PART 19

It had been just under a week since the incident at the Sanhedrin, and repair work was already making excellent progress.

Identifying the reason behind the collapse would be much more time consuming.

Walt Robson was ascending in the building's main lift having been summoned up to see the boss, with the promise of "a breakthrough" regarding the Analyst situation.

You knew when you had reached the directorate floor, because sterile whites and metals gave way to polished solid oak and classical Italian design. Robson always felt a tinge of apprehension when approaching Ezekiel Cleaver's office.

Upon reaching the door he pressed the buzzer, alerting the security camera. The camera whirred as it focussed on the Head of Operations. Robson looked up at it reluctantly, after a couple of seconds the door's lock mechanism audibly disengaged. He pushed the heavy, reinforced door.

Wood furnishing was again replaced by sterile whites, as Robson entered the office.

"Good Morning, Mr Robson, are you well?" Cleaver's rich voice caressed the air of the large space. His impeccably fitting, hand tailored green/grey suit contrasted the white surroundings satisfyingly. Robson returned the salutation as he settled in his seat; he nodded at Felix Baxter who sat to the left of the doctor. Baxter smirked smugly, then looked down at his notepad. "God I hate this little shitbag!" Robson thought to himself.

"How's the Wolf?" Cleaver's tone instead of his fingers provided the air quotes. The question took Robson by surprise somewhat. "Erm, yes we're getting there slowly but surely. Although we've cut off the head, it'll take time for the body to die if you get my meaning," Cleaver nodded slowly. "The Marsh brothers are being predictably tight lipped, and unfortunately Van Hassel, the person we expected to be the most forthcoming...well he's not saying much at all at the moment, due to his mouth being wired shut," he glared at Baxter. The engineer shrugged dismissively. "Wanker," Robson spoke clearly with his eyes. Cleaver looked satisfied "Ok, well I trust you are doing all you can, just keep me up to date". "I will Doctor," Robson confirmed.

Cleaver's face subtly lit up. "Now, on to the reason that I called you here this morning..."

He went on to explain that he had earlier received a phone call from a parliamentary representative, confirming that Cleaver Corp had been granted a private trial and sentencing for Andrew Dax under the Public Interest Immunity principle. The electronic paperwork had followed shortly after.

This not only meant that they could get the defendant tried and charged with little or no outside interference, but

Robson and his team would be free to do their investigations completely unfettered by the media.

"I would like you to deploy one of your best and brightest on this case Mr Robson. You see, on the surface, it would appear that this is an open and shut case. What with the quite clear cut evidence that Mr Baxter here was able to uncover." Cleaver shot a grateful glance in the engineer's direction. "However, as we know, Andrew Dax and the journalist are connected. Needless to say, this could complicate matters somewhat." Cleaver leant in, lowering his voice slightly. "I believe I have completed the first step by ensuring a nice quiet trial.

Now what I need from you is some information around the nature of Dax's relationship with Clyne, but this information will need to be gleaned in a meticulously discreet manner. Do you have someone in mind?" Robson reclined in his seat and rubbed his chin. "Yes I think so".

"Good, good," Cleaver smiled. "How long are we able to keep Dax here in holding?"

Robson grimaced "Not too long, once the trial begins he'll probably be moved to Belmarsh. That is unless they decide to detain him outside London, but we'll do what we can in the time that we have."

The Head of Ops's expression changed from thoughtful to furtive. "Ok, I have a quick question for you, Doctor". Cleaver leant in in anticipation. "Of course".

"Do we have any leads on these random electrocutions? There've been three in the last couple of months and, as you'd expect, questions are being asked. I think I've already explained that one my own men has been indirectly affected by one of these flair ups, and it concerns me that I don't have any answers for him".

Cleaver frowned "Answers? Mr Robson, I sense what you're implying and let me assure you. All we do here at Portentis Power is generate energy, what happens once this energy leaves the complex is down to grid and civil engineers." Robson frowned, but Cleaver continued. "Now please be assured, Portentis take our duty of care in this situation very seriously, and are doing intensive investigations into these isolated incidents. However, and this might surprise you Mr Robson, but random electrical faults leading to injury and even fatality have occurred since the days before Portentis Power!" Cleaver donned a new knowing expression.

"You see, I believe we sometimes forget that electricity, although it is a power source that most take for granted, is still a very awesome and sometimes unpredictable force. A force that, even with mankind's now advanced knowledge thereof, is still a phenomenon which can surprise and inexplicably betray us."

10

Helen sat in her living room, staring down at the readings.

A week ago these crumpled sheets of paper were the most important fixture in the reporter's thinking. However now she had them she felt numb, her senses sedated. What had become of Andrew Dax? Every thought seemed to lead back to this question.

The analyst was originally just a means of getting what she wanted, a passer-by who turned out to be of use to her. Fortunately for her, Dax proved to be a willing and instantly compliant conduit. She imagined that the second she got her hands on the coding, she would immediately be in contact with The Bear.

Now that Dax was gone, leaving her with nothing but a vaguely ominous goodbye note, she couldn't stop thinking about him. She looked over at her phone on the couch beside her. Helen hadn't yet destroyed it as Dax had requested, not because she felt any strong affinity with the device, but because it represented possibly the only means of reengaging with the analyst. She was reminded of the sincerity behind his words: "**for my sake do me a big**

favour and completely destroy the phone carrying this msg asap, please!"

Maybe she should get rid of the phone, maybe by keeping it she was somehow hurting him.

After much back and forth, she decided to decide by the end of the day.

She was struggling to subdue her natural instinct to dig, but intuition told her that she must, at least for now, be still. Her helplessness tormented her.

Reports coming out of the Sanhedrin were that no fatalities were found at the scene. Although this was indeed good news, it didn't help Helen in the near impossible task of piecing together what had happened to Dax that night.

In her heart of hearts she knew that Cleaver Corp lurked in the shadows behind this mystery.

"Andrew, what the hell have they done to you?"

Part 2 (Andrew Dax)

6, 5, 4, 3… 10 YEARS!!… 2, 1. Dax's breathing exercises weren't working today, they kept being interrupted. Every time the panic started to subside, the details of his maximum sentence smashed through his routine like a sounding gong. He sat on the edge of the bunk in the small holding cell which had constituted his home for the last three days; bare walls, a single latrine, and a tiny space. "Wow, nice to see modern prison's interior design has moved on," he had thought to himself upon entry.

The young officer that had provided the death knell seemed sympathetic, but Dax couldn't be sure if this was genuine. It may have been a ploy to trip him up, sort of like the good cop minus the bad cop. During this time Dax had remained silent, successfully stifling the urge to blurt out clichés such as "I DIDN'T DO IT!" or "I'M BEING

FRAMED!" This was by far the wrong person to divulge these revelations to.

The possible 10 year maximum sentence was touched on by the young officer who had booked him in upon arrival at Central Enforcements. He also explained to Dax why he had been arrested, as the zombie cop was unable to do so. The living cop also informed Dax of his options around legal representation.

The slow release seep of anxiety was proving impossible to close off.

The irony of the term "office prisoner" flickered in his mind mockingly.

Dax was way past the "this can't be happening!" stage, and was now securely locked in the box labelled "creeping dread."

———

UPON ARRIVAL to the holding division, the officer had asked him who he would like notified of his arrest.

Dax chose his mother. He was not allowed to make the contact himself. The cop had also informed him that he was not permitted to make contact with anyone outside the Sanhedrin walls until the aforementioned legal representation arrived.

"Why can't I make my own phone call?" Dax thought to himself.

"Something's wrong here." He rubbed his head at the horrible understatement of the situation.

Dax's vision began to wobble and fade, the panic had grown beyond the prospect of reversal and terror now prevailed.

He'd had bad attacks before, the intense and sudden flight response prevailing at a moment's notice. But this felt more all-encompassing, more final.

Dax's pores began to ooze with cold perspiration. His heart hammered so rapidly and intensely that he could have sworn it was externally audible, his chest began to tighten. Dax fell to his knees, now taking massive panicked breaths. Flares of pain soared up and down his left arm and his throat narrowed, allowing only small seeps of oxygen to enter his struggling lungs. Dax knew he was in trouble. He tried to cry out for help, but all that registered were tiny pathetic whimpers.

That familiar "permanent sleep" feeling washed over him.

He needed to get to the cell door, in order to rap on it and scream for assistance. But as he crawled forward looking up, the door began to fade from vision. Dax's hammering heart faltered and tripped, the pain in his chest became unbearable, he cried out...

Then all was black.

PART 3 (CLYNE/CARTWRIGHT)

The short, sharp knock at the door startled Helen.

She wasn't expecting visitors, and family- although they did tend to turn up randomly- had never paid her an impromptu visit at 8:30 on a Saturday morning. Helen was an early riser, and was relieved that today she had decided to get dressed straight away. As she jogged down the stairs a thought occurred to her, a thought that filled her with a sudden surge of nervous anticipation: "It's Andrew!" By the time she'd finished her descent and took in the male, medium build silhouette at her door, she was absolutely convinced it was the analyst. She slowly opened the door a few inches, leaving the latch engaged.

It wasn't Dax.

Instead it was extremely handsome man with piercing blue eyes, ultra-defined cheek bones and dusty blond, slightly unruly hair. Helen's immediate guess would have placed him in his late twenties.

"Good morning Ms Clyne?"

Helen neither confirmed nor denied, but bounced a question back. "And you are?"

"Oh sorry, I'm Officer Tom Cartwright, Operations at Central Enforcements."

He showed her his ID, although Helen had already guessed he was a police man.

She confirmed her identity.

"I'd like to ask you a few questions around the Drone malfunction incidents 8 weeks ago. Is this a good time?"

"As good as any I guess."

No one really likes talking to the police, but at least Helen had had slightly more experience at it than most, being in the media.

Helen invited Cartwright inside, as she led him down the hallway into her living room, she tried to keep her instant attraction to him disguised but she had never been very good at this. However she had a feeling the task would get easier as their conversation developed.

Cartwright settled into the small armchair in the corner of the space.

"Ok so, there are a couple of things I have to make you aware of before I continue."

Helen shrugged.

Cartwright got out a notepad and squinted at it, then looked up and continued.

"He doesn't do this a lot," Helen thought to herself, noticing the officer's unsure demeanour.

"The case in question is being investigated under the Public Interest Immunity act, this means…"

"It means that the second you start asking what you came here to ask, I become simultaneously subject to a gagging order," Helen cut the officer off boldly.

Cartwright raised an eyebrow.

"I'm a journalist!" Helen reminded.

"Yes, well, it's not technically a gagging order as such."

Helen sighed. "Yeah, right ok"

Helen's attitude had clearly rattled the young officer, as

he fumbled and skipped through the rest of the explanation.

Cartwright was slightly annoyed by his lack of control of the exchange and reasserted himself.

"I want to know the nature of your relationship with Andrew Dax," he said sternly.

Helen attempted to hide her alarm at the mention of the name. She prepared herself for the dance.

"And if I told you that the name meant nothing to me?"

"I would say you were lying."

Helen raised her eyebrows. "And what would make you say that?"

Cartwright paused and stared at the journalist. "We've been monitoring Dax."

Helen frowned. "Oh so it's Dax you've been monitoring…*DAX*?" Helen over pronounced the surname knowingly.

Cartwright felt exposed. He sensed that she knew this was a lie.

"Andrew Dax is a person of interest in our investigations into the fatal drone malfunctions."

Helen frowned, "a person of interest, you mean you've arrested him?"

"He's a person of interest, that's all I'm at liberty to disclose at this point. But what I will say, is that just as you are legally obligated to treat all conversations related to this case as classified, you are also legally obligated to assist us with our investigation to the best of your ability."

Helen chuckled to herself, "my ability to assist is somewhat stifled by your cagey and vague drip feed of information. I don't fly blind very well."

Helen sighed.

"Ok, Andrew's just a friend, a fellow writer of sorts, I know he works at the Sanhedrin, but I don't really understand the intricacies of his role." Helen felt satisfied at the convincing nature of the lie.

"I'm pretty sure he has nothing to do with drones though. In fact I think they freak him out a little." Helen smirked.

"You don't genuinely believe he's behind this do you?"

"I'm not at liberty to divulge that," Cartwright confirmed.

Helen rolled her eyes, "Well this is a wonderful conversation, I'm glad I woke up early for it! Ok, so I've answered your first question, are there anymore or is that it?"

PART 20

Mr Dax?

Mr Dax!

Mr Dax, Can you hear me?

The voice progressed through the tunnel of his consciousness.

Lucidity was returning to Dax, his vision began to clear.

The man that emerged was smooth-faced, steely-eyed and fifty-ish. His severe hair cut seemed to shout the analyst out of his stupor.

Dax began to take in his surroundings. He was in one of the medical rooms at Central Enforcements.

His first feeling was that of relief in the fact that he was alive. This feeling was quickly succeeded by the regret of waking up in the same horrible situation.

"What… what happened?" Dax groaned, dragging himself up to a sitting position on the bed.

Smooth-face's steely eyes softened a shade. "You had a

severe anxiety attack, followed by a panic induced black-out.

Dax remembered the pain in his chest that had radiated down his left arm. "My heart!"

The man smiled. "All your vitals are fine. I have it on good authority that the severest panic attacks can often mimic more serious health emergencies. For instance, strokes or heart attacks."

Dax's weary senses reluctantly returned to him. While the pain in his chest and left arm had indeed subsided, all his muscles ached as if he had just completed a triathlon. He was exhausted.

"And you are?" the analyst croaked.

"Oh yes, my name is Robert Beckman. I'm the legal professional assigned to your case, the medic will be back shortly to check on you, but he is confident that you are fine, physically."

Smooth-face could see that Dax was still a little out of it.

"I just popped over to introduce myself."

"I'll be back tomorrow, when you're feeling better, and we can have our first full consultation. You did confirm that you were without your own legal representation, didn't you?"

Dax rubbed his head, "Erm yeah, yeah."

The lawyer got up. "Well let me assure you Mr Dax, I am a highly trained criminal, legal professional with over 20 years of experience within the field.

I actually specialise in criminal negligence and involuntary manslaughter."

The label smashed through Dax's daze like a wrecking ball…*CRIMINAL!*

His eyes widened.

At that moment he knew that his life had genuinely

changed forever. How the hell could a jury be persuaded that he was an innocent party in this mess?

Cleaver Corp ate nobodies like him for brunch (even less significant than breakfast). As soon as this Beckman character started to paw through what Dax presumed was an immaculately formed set of cyber-evidence, he would immediately change tack, and opt for a shorter sentence. He would class that as a success in this particular case.

Smooth-face didn't wait for a response, but strolled to the door and pressed the buzzer to be released.

As the thick security door hissed shut, the undeniable fact burned through all else in Dax's mangled thinking: "There's only one person that can save me now!"

11

"Wha's his name? Get his ID out!" One of the gang shouted.

Another member grabbed Kai Phipps's jacket, lifting his limp body slightly, then ripped his ID from within.

As his body was dropped back to the tarmac, Phipps let out a muffled whimper.

"Officer Kai Phipps…"

"Kai Phipps? HA HA… what kinda batty-hole name is dat man!?" The five boys laughed gleefully.

40 minutes ago, Phipps had been called out to a routine residential disturbance. He had gone against the new rule that no officer was to respond to this kind of callout alone. Kai Phipps was now learning the hard way why this rule had been agreed, due to the lack of Drone back up.

It was a trap.

As the officer approached the address, a gang of five youths had set upon him. One was armed with a length of steel pipe.

And now Phipps lay, prostrate. Three broken ribs, a

shattered collar bone, a fractured skull and severe internal bleeding were his punishment for disobeying the new rule.

And they weren't finished.

"You ain't got ya robots to come save ya now have ya piggy?" The question was rhetorical.

The sheer agony Phipps was experiencing made him pray for the escape that only the loss of consciousness could bring. At this point he considered begging for his life to be spared.

Suddenly he had a flash of his life, up to this moment. All of that effort to make the grade, all the late nights, all the extra training. Why? To be a better peacekeeper and protect the public more efficiently. All that, only to end here, face down in the street, on a rundown estate at the arse end of Hackney. A 34 year old police officer, beaten to death by children…how embarrassing!

At that moment Phipps decided that if it was to end here, whether to whimper futile pleas for mercy or not, would be one of the last choices he would ever make.

He decided against it.

Phipps' rolling eyes focussed for just long enough to see the trainer swing back… SLAM!

The kick was square in the face. Phipps heard his teeth groan as they loosened.

A giggle came from above. "Oh shit!" one of them sniggered.

The trainer swung back again… SLAM!

Four teeth exploded from the officer's ruined face, a fifth tooth was stopped by his top lip and stayed imbedded there.

The mocking voices above echoed then stuttered…

The escape of unconsciousness finally arrived.

PART 21

- **What do you mean you've lost him?**
- **I think the Corp have arrested him.**
- **I thought he was straight?**
- **I think he is. My guess is they're trying to frame him for the Drone malfunctions. Had a cop round asking questions, but he wouldn't give anything away about his whereabouts.**
- **Well I need him, and you need to bring him to me.**
- **But I don't know where he is!**
- **Sorry, no Dax, no decoding.**
- **That wasn't the deal!**
- **The deal has changed.**
- **I'm willing to double the amount I'm paying you.**
- **You don't get it do you? This thing is bigger than you.**

"Bastard!" Helen cried out, slamming her fist down on the desk, making the keyboard jump forwards towards her.

The Bear had been inexplicably interested in Andrew Dax ever since she'd mentioned meeting him weeks ago. On more than one occasion he had grilled her on what she knew of Dax's technical abilities and she had at that stage, given him the fullness of her limited knowledge. Helen had always found The Bear mysterious and labyrinthine, and at first she just assumed this interrogation regarding Dax was a competitive thing.

However, more recently the hacker had been speaking of "the bigger picture" and "the long game" and he now seemed intent on recruiting the analyst as his right-hand man. Helen's intuition told her that Dax was being held at Central Enforcements but she couldn't be certain. Even if she did know of Dax's whereabouts, the Bear seemed to assume the analyst would instantly drop everything and join forces with him. Helen wasn't so sure.

Now the hacker was holding her to ransom. Dax, for the decoding she so desperately needed. Her life was literally on hold until she had these.

The confirmation of Portentis' part in her brother's death, her hard-hitting campaign to blow the lid off this cover up, the dozens that could be spared the grim fate her brother had faced, none of this could even start until she had that decoding.

Helen was tired of feeling helpless.

PART 22

"Alright people, listen up!" Robson shouted, clapping his hands to get his team's attention. "Everyone, pull up a pew."

The atmosphere at Central Enforcements had been much more intense over the last couple of months. Having to pick up the slack left behind by the Com Cops, meant the department had to work extra hours and at a much faster rate. However, noises coming from the directorate were that the pressure could be eased sooner rather than later.

The sombre expression on the Chief's face made the group settle a little quicker than usual.

"I come bearing bad news, I'm afraid. Phipps was jumped last night. He went against new protocol, and went on a disturbance callout alone."

A concerned mumble moved through the group.

"He's at Newham and he's in a really bad way by all accounts. Only relatives are being allowed to see him at the moment. So you know it ain't good."

The mumble re-emerged.

"Shut up!" Robson shouted.

"Regulations, even new ones, are laid down for a reason people! Rightly or wrongly, we're a department that is no longer equipped to take these kinds of calls without back up. Meaning no Com Cops, no lone responses! And that goes for every cop shop in the city."

"When can he have visitors?" One of the group spoke up.

"I don't know, but I think the focus for the next 24 hours at least, will be on keeping the poor sod alive."

Robson moved over to the large screen at the far end of the space, took the controller device and switched the monitor on.

"Now, although Phipps' actions were idiotic in the extreme, he did have the presence of mind to turn his Identi- Scanner on before it happened."

A montage of young faces shuffled on the screen.

"Now these little scumbags are the culprits. A group of 14 to 19 year olds from down Hackney end, they call themselves the Hants Hill Mob. I want everyone to blow the dust off those very expensive Identi-Pads of yours and sync them with these images."

The group moved about frantically, each looking for their own, underused device.

"Until we catch every last one of these little shits no one goes anywhere without their Identi-Pad. Have we got that?"

There was no answer. Thunder suddenly marked Robson's face.

"I SAID HAVE WE GOT THAT?!" The chief boomed.

"Yes chief!" the team answered in unison.

As the group dispersed Robson made a bee-line for Tom Cartwright and tapped him on the shoulder.

Cartwright turned. "How are you getting on with your Commissar Control training? I may need you on standby, with what's happened with Phipps."

The young officer frowned, his mind was elsewhere. "Erm yeah, I actually finished a couple days ago, so yeah I'm ready to go!" Cartwright's plastic smile didn't fool the chief.

"How is she, son?" he whispered, his face softening with concern.

Cartwright sighed "Erm not good chief, they've called us all in tonight, and that's never a good sign. I clock off around now, so I'll be on my way there shortly. I can't say I'm looking forward to it to be honest." Robson rubbed the young officer's shoulder, "I can imagine." He looked down and shook his head "There are things that happen in this life that just make no sense whatsoever, and fairness? Well fairness just don't come into it. But at the very least you and the family can get some closure."

Cartwright closed his eyes and nodded.

"If there's anything I can do, anything at all, you let me know."

Cartwright nodded again.

Robson smiled warmly, "I mean it son"

Cartwright had always admired the way his boss could make such a seamless transition between booming drill sergeant and attentive counsellor at the drop of a hat.

"I know you do sir, thanks."

Part 4 (Legal Eagle)

Consultation Room 1 seemed to shrink a little more every time Dax looked around.

A cold steel desk and two plastic moulded chairs provided the only furnishing in the sterile space.

Robert Beckman –"Legal Eagle"- sat opposite the

analyst staring down at the gathered files, periodically grimacing and making subtle "tutting" sounds to himself.

Andrew Dax had just finished detailing the intricacies of his job. Then he was asked to run through everything he knew about Com Cops – that part didn't take too long.

Then, with great difficulty, he did his best to recollect his actions and whereabouts on the week of the killings.

The lawyer continued to bow at the documents. He hadn't said anything for several minutes. Dax summoned all his legal knowledge, and came to the conclusion that this was a bad thing.

The sustained quiet allowed the subtle seep of anxiety begin to re-escape in Dax.

"Has he forgotten I'm here?" he wondered.

The lawyer looked up from the papers, but still said nothing.

Finally, a conspiratorial smirk lit his face, he leant in towards Dax.

"You're one of these "Digital Activists" aren't you?" he said, almost in a whisper.

Dax frowned, but the lawyer continued. "You wouldn't be the first, believe me." He chuckled to himself. "I mean, you wouldn't even be the first that was employed within these walls!"

"I get the fact that not everyone is enjoying Cleaver's London, you know."

The lawyer was whispering now. "Come on, if you were to tell me that you're some kind of freedom fighter, then, believe it or not, it will make my job a lot easier."

Dax's frown deepened. "Are you serious? Have you heard a word I've said? And what kind of cause would I be upholding by reprogramming giant robots to kill random members of the public?"

Beckman rubbed his chin. "All I'm saying is, if we could muddy the waters somewhat on the whys and wherefores that might give us some wiggle room in maybe having a stab at a "good cause gone wrong" kind of angle."

Anxiety gave way to anger in Dax.

"Oh ok, so now we're not even considering the crazy notion that I might be innocent? Forensics? Lie detection? Are you telling me there's no way at all to put forward the case that someone's screwing me over?!"

"Mr Dax…"

"No!" Dax shouted over the lawyer. He leapt up from his seat and began pacing frantically. "Who the hell are you, anyway? You're no help whatsoever!" Dax was rabbling now and rubbing his head. "Wait, what the hell was I thinking, of course you're no help! *They've* sent you! I want to change my lawyer right now!"

Beckman had seen this panicked paranoia before, in condemned men. He softened his voice in an attempt to calm his client.

"Mr Dax, please listen to me. I'm here to defend you, that's what I'm paid to do. I assure you I have no allegiance to anyone but myself, and, by extension, my next pay packet, which takes the form of you right now.

If you are adamant that you're an innocent party in this, then that is exactly what I will attempt to prove."

Dax sat down and stared at the lawyer.

"But I do have to let you know that this evidence is pretty damning. All was saying was that if there's anything you're not telling me…anything at all. It's best you spill now."

Part 5 (Grief, Interrupted)

Tom Cartwright sat at the wheel of his car in silence.

For the first time that night, hot tears began to stream down his cheeks. He had held it together at the chapel of rest, sensing that it was important to be strong for his mum and dad.

Kim Cartwright, Tom's sister, was on the way home from a wine tasting course in Central London with her partner, Claire. As they approached their home in Stepney, they were attacked by a local man who attempted to mug them. The assailant was then inexplicably electrocuted by an underground power surge. As the couple attempted to escape the scene, the dying man leapt upon Kim, sending the charge through her, resulting in severe high voltage electrical burns to 70 per cent of her body. The impact of her head hitting the floor resulted in severe cranial trauma. This plunged Kim into a deep coma. She had remained in this state for the last three weeks.

At 8:47pm tonight, Kim Cartwright's life support was switched off and her body was laid in the chapel of rest at Newham University Hospital.

She was 23 years old.

Tom was never that close to his sister, but he loved her. The regret for words unsaid began to swell.

He knew that Kim wasn't going to survive upon first laying eyes on her at the hospital.

However, having time to prepare for the inevitable didn't make the event any more palatable.

His sister was dead, his job was slowly becoming obsolete, soon to be replaced by recycled criminals, and his colleague lay savaged and clinging to life just yards from where he sat, in the self-same hospital.

Another figure simmered in his mind, just under the thick layer of grief. His brief encounter with the condemned analyst had left him troubled. He prided himself on being a quick and efficient judge of guilt and something just didn't sit right with this one.

He started to sense a common factor.

Tom Cartwright's mind swam.

"What the hell is happening to this city?"

Had the company that employed him, become the monkey on the back of the very city it was supposed to be supporting?

He rubbed his face vigorously in order to compose himself.

He selfishly just wanted to be alone, but he had promised his inconsolable mother he would stay with his parents tonight, so they could comfort each other.

The Cartwright's only ever had two children, and as people, they didn't boast much emotional strength.

Cartwright pulled away to begin the drive to his parents' North London home.

12

T he cool, smooth surface of the cell door satisfied Felix Baxter's fingertips.

The engineer caressed the surface up and down gently with his left hand. He paused, leaned in and slowly placed his ear against the door, listening intently for a moment. However, no stirring emerged from within. "This is how I will make my name," he confirmed to himself.

Although Baxter had clearance for most of the Sanhedrin building, he had "acquired" his access to the holding section tonight. He'd chosen a typically quiet time, when only the night guards were on the clock.

He was in a playful mood.

Taking the handle to the viewing slot between his fingers, he slid the hatch open, but didn't immediately peer in.

"Dax," he whispered. There was no answer.

"Dax," he repeated, only marginally louder. He heard stirring from within.

His anticipation grew.

"Dax," he called again, raising his voice, but again only

slightly. Although he felt bold, he didn't want to draw unnecessary attention.

"Ugh… hello?" the voice from within was gruff and slumbering.

It was time for a peek.

The holding cell was a small, cramped looking space. As Baxter's eyes adjusted to the gloom within, he began to make out the shape of the analyst, as he shifted uncomfortably on his pathetic little bunk.

"Who's there?" the voice from within mumbled. The dim light flicked on.

"It's your whistle blower"

Dax stood, rubbed his eyes and shuffled towards the door, squinting out. "Felix?"

The engineer smiled. "That's me! My word, you've been a naughty boy, haven't you? And you'd have gotten away with it too, if it wasn't for this meddling engineer!"

Dax had now come around fully. "You mean this…all this is your doing?"

Baxter smiled. "Well I couldn't let you get away with it, could I? I mean, you're a killer!"

Dax realised he was being taunted and did his best not to rise to the bait. "I'm not a killer, and when my trial begins, I'm going to prove it," he confirmed calmly.

"Oh yes, the "secret trial", that starts in a couple of weeks, doesn't it? That whole no contact with the outside world thing. That must be tough, aye? Didn't even seem legal to me at first, but I read up on it, and it turns out it bloody well is!" Baxter chuckled "It's absolutely frigging watertight! I tell you, that Cleaver's a vicious bastard, but you've got to hand it to him. He's an absolute genius-they've got you completely by the balls on this one!"

The truth in the statement stung Dax painfully.

The engineer sniggered again.

"Oh yes, and I've heard they're moving you to the big

boy prison soon, too. Oh and you know how jailbirds feel about inmates that kill kids!" Baxter shuddered theatrically.

Dax pressed his eyes shut, attempting to repress the urge to grab what he could of the little weasel and tear it through the tiny gap.

"What are you doing down here, Baxter? Has your very last friend abandoned you up there, so you thought you'd try your luck down here? Captive audience and all that?"

Baxter smiled but persevered. "Do you know how much trouble you're in? You're looking at a proper stretch here mate!"

Dax rolled his eyes. "Seriously Baxter, if you're looking to cruise, you're really better off down that "big boy" prison you mentioned, more of a varied selection."

Part 2 (Mr & Mrs Dax)

"Held? What do you mean held? Why, what has he done?"

Audrey Dax had started the conversation in a relatively calm manner. This was in keeping with her personality. She also knew from past experience that going in "all guns blazing" would make people of this ilk clam up even more so than they already had. However, at this point, frustration and concern for her son was beginning to overwhelm her. This wasn't helped by the disaffected, monotone style in which the Central Enforcement Clerk met each of her enquiries.

"I appreciate your concern, however, because of the sensitivity of the case, it has been classified as confidential. At this stage I cannot disclose any details to you or anyone else who is not directly connected."

Colin and Audrey Dax had been summoned to this appointment in response to their determined and repeated calls the offices, enquiring about their son's whereabouts. They had obviously become very concerned at Andrew's apparent disappearance, and become suspicious at his employer's evasive stance of neither confirming nor denying that their son was on site. Now they sat before the young Clerk in the chilly general enquires area of Central Enforcements, exchanging several words but getting nowhere. Audrey tended to be the spokesperson of the couple, as her husband was a painfully shy and reserved man. Colin Dax fidgeted and wrung his hands in a worried fashion.

"This is nonsense, I'm not having this. I mean, this can't be legal!" Audrey Dax leant forward and looked beyond the Clerk. "I want to speak to someone in charge, now! Who's in charge of this so-called case?" The Clerk grimaced in anticipation of her reaction. "I'm afraid that, at this point you cannot speak to anyone directly connected to the case." Audrey Dax slumped back in her seat and sighed gravely. The Clerk was trying, and failing, to appear sympathetic. "This won't be forever, and believe me your son is absolutely safe. As soon as we are able, we'll be in touch with more information."

Colin Dax finally spoke, "So that's it, is it? We're just supposed to go home and act like this isn't happening?"

The clerk sighed, leaned in and lowered his voice, "Of course not. Look, I'm not even supposed to tell you this, but try to be satisfied, for now at least, that this isn't rape or paedophilia or anything gross like that.

Your son works for the policing governing body for this city, and as such, I'm afraid you're just going to have to accept that the details of certain projects and operations cannot be disclosed to you until an appropriate stage. I promise that he is safe and you will be contacted as soon as we are procedurally able."

PART 23

Did you really think all that intel was free of charge?

No, but that's why I'm offering more money

I don't need money, I need the Analyst! Besides I thought you said he was innocent?

We're getting ahead of ourselves, I said I "guess" he's being held and I "think" he's innocent. Even if what I'm guessing is true, and I was about to put my freedom and career on the line for two people I don't even know! How the hell do I go about breaking someone out of the Sanhedrin?!

It's not as complicated as you might think, besides you would only have to get him outside of the walls, I would do the rest.

"Baxter, you little rat faced scumbag!" Dax flung the steel tray against the wall of his cell, coating it in a star shape of tepid, slimy potato and bland mystery-meat stew.

Because the Sanhedrin was only equipped with a small number of short stay - holding cells, it didn't have the communal eating areas of which larger, made for purpose prisons boasted. For the last two hellish weeks Dax's meals had been delivered directly to his cell in metal - TV dinner style trays.

The shallow "clang" of the silver hitting the wall, prompted hurried footsteps. The viewing slot slid open, "not hungry today aye, nerdy?" Dax didn't look up but recognised the shrill, nasal voice of a particularly obnoxious guard. Wilson or something, Dax didn't care enough to remember.

"Well I hope you like the smell of rotting food, coz I aint facking cleaning it up!" The slot snapped shut.

Felix Baxter had paid him a visit last night. In the main, the engineer had stopped by to let Dax know that it was he that had highlighted the data which ultimately led to his arrest. The rest of the exchange was centred around taunting on Baxter's part.

Dax buried his face in his hands. He'd never liked or indeed trusted Felix Baxter, and he assumed the feeling was pretty much mutual but there was no way he could ever have imagined that the engineer would betray him to the extent of robbing Dax of his freedom. And all just to take the spotlight off himself!

Less than a month ago, before Helen Clyne, before all this, Dax's only real problems were mild job disillusionment and the odd panic attack here and there. Problems that he was quite sure were shared by many. Now here he sat, the only suspect in a triple manslaughter case, completely cut off from family and friends, suffering terrifying faux-heart attacks and being moved around like a pawn by a mad scientist and a snivelling engineer... a lot can change in 4 weeks!

"But how the hell did he do it?" Dax couldn't work out whether he'd just been completely naïve to Baxter's soft programming skills or if he had worked with a skilled accomplice. He remembered the panicked engineer in his office, frantically pawing through the engine readings. Was the plan hatched directly after this?

Cleaver Corp needed a figurehead for the drone malfunctions, as this was the organisation's only hope of getting the machines re-commissioned and back on the streets. In the days that followed the incidents, Andrew considered the notion that they might try to scapegoat someone, but not even in his deepest, darkest nightmares did he guess that he would be that scapegoat!

Part 5 (Grief, Interrupted)

The streets hadn't looked this foreboding in years. Shadows were darker, the air was thicker and adjacent buildings leaned in imposingly. Grudging truth began to emerge from graffiti tagged walls from:

"CLEAVER'S LONDON'S BURNING!"

to

"Doctor Doom"

Cartwright drove somewhat on auto-pilot across town. He'd just finished the A roads part of his journey back from his overnight stay at his parents' home in Enfield. He was making steady progress through a dark, dank Homerton. Cartwright glanced down at his car's time piece: 9:42pm.

The image of his withered sister still burned in his mind like corrosive acid.

He hadn't noticed the huddled group on the pavement beside him as he stopped at the traffic lights, that is at least until he heard a soft beeping sound from inside his coat. The sound snapped the officer out of his malaise. He ripped the Identi-Pad from his inside pocket and pulled the car over. The device had made a direct match with one of the suspects in Kai Phipps' attack.

A pale, pig-nosed boy with ginger hair and hateful green eyes stared back at Cartwright from the small monitor. Cartwright snarled and looked around him. The device was indicating that the 15 year old was part of the huddled group to his right. He suddenly remembered that he was off duty and alone, but he didn't care. What was the point in carrying the Identi-Pad around everywhere, if you couldn't act once it had made a positive match?

He would indeed act, but he knew he had to be smart. The redhead was the only suspect in the group, this aided Cartwright with containment. Plus the car the officer was driving was unmarked and rather fortuitously the device had gone off in almost perfect synchronisation with the boy exchanging hand salutations with his crew. Then he broke from the group, making his way down a side street.

Cartwright waited a few seconds in the gloom behind the wheel. The rest of the group disbanded. He pulled away slowly in subtle pursuit of the boy, leaving his headlights off.

As he turned down the narrow one-way street, the redhead came into view. The lad didn't turn.

Cartwright remembered the dying thug that had ultimately killed his sister, the dead-eyed savagery that his colleague and friend had been subjected to, less than 48 hours ago. And here this kid strode confidently, as if nothing had happened!

Melancholy turned to rage.

The car rolled forward, almost silently. "Taser!" he

whispered, as he rummaged around in the glove compartment searching for the gun, keeping one eye on his target. He grabbed the pair of handcuffs he kept in the door compartment and shoved them into his inside pocket.

He then located and grabbed the weapon, brought the car to an abrupt halt and burst from the vehicle.

"Stop! Police!" Cartwright roared as he loaded the cartridge into the weapon and hurled himself at the boy. The redhead didn't even turn to face his pursuer, but took up an immediate sprint.

Cartwright slowed to a jog in order to steady himself and take aim. "Don't make me fire!" he barked as a final warning. The panting boy slowed and half turned but didn't stop, Cartwright was glad, as he wanted to inflict pain on this little monster.

He aimed the laser point between the boy's shoulder blades and fired. Cartwright didn't see the barb leave the weapon but a surprised, high pitch sound exploding from his target confirmed the hit – a cross between a barking dog and a manic yodel.

Cartwright slowly lowered the Taser gun and began to walk towards the stricken hoody. As he took the cuffs from his inside pocket, he prepared to make the boy aware of his rights - then stopped dead in his tracks.

The officer noticed a strangled gagging sound emitting from the boy. His outstretched arms began to tremble, his stiffening body turned to face him. Cold and hate filled eyes had been transformed into pools of unbridled terror. A hot electrical aroma laced the air. The boy began to convulse violently.

Cartwright was caught between confusion and panic "this isn't a reaction to the Taser shot!"

He then remembered his conversation with the grieving Claire Armitage. At that moment he realised what was happening.

The boy howled in agony as smoke began to emerge from under his clothes and his skin glowed orange-red against the night. He was burning from within.

"GAHH, GROOG, ARGH!" the boy was trying to speak as he staggered towards the young officer, arms outstretched, pleadingly.

The boy was doomed. Anger turned to guilt as Cartwright realised he would have to run in order to survive.

The staggering boy picked up speed, his skin now blackened and charring. Flecks of light, like sparks, began to spit from his burning fingers, as he suddenly found another gear. He galloped towards the momentarily trans-fixed police man, now mere feet away.

Cartwright felt the intense heat emitting from the burning boy, as he cried out again and fell forward, hands flailing, inches from the officer's chest.

Cartwright yelped involuntarily, as he spun and ran, attempting to make it to the safety of his car, untouched.

Part 6 (Ezekiel Cleaver)

Ezekiel Cleaver, the master problem solver, felt good.

He felt better than he had done in months. Correc-tional work on the complex was making excellent progress, and the public statement had been put forward and swal-lowed whole.

The reason given was "structural weakness." Of course, this rather vague explanation would have been greeted with much more scrutiny if the incident had claimed any lives. But it hadn't – problem solved.

The troublemaking analyst had been arrested and was due to be moved to Belmarsh, where his bail arrangements and trial would begin –problem solved.

Sark, Abercrombie and two other Commissars were

due to be officially unveiled on the 2nd of December (today was the 22nd of November). Plus, with a satisfactory explanation and culprit for the tragedies, it wouldn't be too long before his drones were back on the streets.

Bringing the city's slowly elevating crime rates back down – problem solved.

The physicist sat back in the soft, Italian leather recliner in the second sitting room of his mansion. For the first time in almost a year he had allowed himself a couple of days off.

Cleaver didn't often take holidays abroad, or even venture to any of his abodes in the US or Europe. The amount miles he accumulated in a year meant that most of his down time was spent here in Hertfordshire.

Of course down time in Cleaver's case was a term used rather loosely. As he was, right now flicking through some of his multi-faceted organisation's annual numbers. He wanted to get his charitable donation figures confirmed and sent to the Finance Department by the end of the day.

This was one of a handful of the conglomerate's budgetary decisions that Cleaver kept full ownership of.

13

PART 1 (UNINVITED GUEST)

BANG, BANG,BANG! The front door creaked with the force of the knocks.

Helen Clyne shot bolt upright in her bed, wide-eyed, breathing shallowly.

As she looked at the time piece on the bedside cabinet to her right, an explosion of dread coursed through her entire body... 10:34pm... "Who the hell is that?!" she panted out loud.

Violent crime and burglary had made an almost endemic rise in her area of late. Helen was no wimp, but she knew when to pick her battles. She put on her dressing gown and slightly parted the curtains, trying to get a glimpse of her visitor.

Helen knew that if it wasn't Dax on the other side of her front door, then she was in real trouble!

She grabbed her mobile phone from the dresser and crept out of her room, pushing 999 and leaving her finger over the CALL button as she peeped down the stairs into the gloom below.

Knock... knock. The sound was softer and more pleading

this time. She turned on every light available as she appre-
hensively descended the staircase.

The silhouette that stood in the darkness seemed
agitated.

Helen stopped her approach a safe distance from the
door "Who's there?" she asked, unable to mask the
nervousness in her voice.

"I… it's Cartwright…Officer Cartwright." The voice
sounded shaky and distressed.

"What do you want?" Helen enquired suspiciously.

"I need to talk to you…. please!" The pleading tone
seemed genuine.

Helen slowly opened the door a few inches, leaving the
chain engaged. The young officer's blue eyes were hollow
and haunted. He leant against the wall panting.

Cartwright didn't wait for her to speak. "Wha-what
happened to your brother?" he asked, voice still shaky with
distress.

Part 2 (Justice Looms)

The legend of Sark and Abercrombie is moving through
the organised crime world like folklore.

Small shards of the full picture are all that have been
filtered down thus far.

Nevertheless, news has been spreading fast of the swift
and brutal take down of the core cell of the Wolf pack.
Two blank eyed, sharp suited agents of uncontainable law
enforcement have now strolled boldly into the consciousness. The sudden and ruthlessly efficient manner in which
these two mysterious men were able to overcome five of
the most dangerous men in Europe, has even the slickest of
the hard-core spooked. You can't counter what you don't
understand.

The theories are many and varied, some more out-there than others.

Organised crime hasn't ceased to exist overnight. But what's for sure is that since the night the Wolf got made, strategic meetings involving key decision makers have taken place far outside of the capital.

The almost completely unpublicised and sudden manner in which Sark and Abercrombie were introduced had the exact effect that Cleaver Corp desired. Even if the balance of nervousness amongst the criminal underbelly is shared with the general public, because of the current depleted nature of the police force and the slow rise in random violent crime. The prospect of more Commissars, plus the possible re-commissioning of the Com Cops could soon make London almost impenetrable to criminality.

Soon the ominous spectre of that black private ambulance (which is the chosen cover vehicle for the duo) looming over the horizon, will spark dread into the most fearsome of felons.

PART 24

The coffee was warm and rich in flavour; it was obviously a brand of high quality.

Unfortunately, Tom Cartwright's senses were only firing on a couple of cylinders, making the enjoyment incomplete.

The officer's shaking hands had calmed somewhat, enabling him to lift the mug to his lips and taste the warm brew that Helen had prepared for him.

Upon being given the assignment of grilling the reporter to find out what she knew of Andrew Dax, Cartwright did some of his own digging on the journalist.

He had begun this, just days after his sister's attack. When you're feeling that level of helplessness, sometimes work is the only remedy.

However, what he discovered turned out to be more of an irritant than an elixir.

The journalist too had recently lost a sibling to a vaguely explained "freak accident." And while Kim Cartwright's life still hung in the balance, Robert Clyne died instantly from reported electrocution. At the time of reading this, Cartwright's rational mind told him that Robert Clyne could have been an Electrician, a Building Contractor or even a Civil Engineer, and that was to name but a few. Any of the aforementioned career paths could have ended in this kind of abrupt tragedy.

However he couldn't shake the feeling that there was a connection.

Researching the journalist's private life had left Cartwright sufficiently intrigued; what he had seen tonight had confirmed his need to know more. A lot more.

Witnessing a person spontaneously combust was, Cartwright guessed, less likely than winning the lottery two times in succession. However, there Cartwright sat, shoulders hunched, in the corner of Helen Clyne's living room having, less than an hour ago seen a child burn to death from within.

Helen wasn't in the practice of letting strange men into her home at night – no matter how cute. She also didn't suffer fools gladly. Upon taking in the young officer's haunted expression as he blurted out that first question, she knew that something awful linked them. Hearing the tragic story of Kim Cartwright, along with the account of the horror he had witnessed tonight, confirmed that link.

The young officer's once olive skin was pale and ashen.

Explaining in detail what had happened to Robbie didn't seem to help the policeman's mood.

"What the hell is happening to this city?" He asked the question more to the room than to Helen, eyes vacant and lost.

Helen leaned forward and clasped her hands together. "I think you know," she said quietly.

Cartwright looked into the reporter's eyes. "Cleaver," he whispered.

"Indirectly, I think so, yes," Helen nodded "Now don't

get me wrong. This matter or organism that powers Portentisis undoubtedly revolutionary. And I still believe it could one day be the answer to the global energy shortage. However I still don't think enough is known about it. I'm not certain whether or not these electrical flare ups are directly related to Portentis Power, but if Cleaver had any doubts about its stability, it shouldn't have been installed."

Cartwright's eyes widened. "Something needs to be done now, why isn't anyone acting NOW?!"

"You're asking me? He's your boss!" Helen found a subtle smile.

"Don't you need to call it in or something?" she asked, diverting the conversation, as she knew there was no immediate resolve to the one previous.

"I already have. I just reported it as a disturbance. I'm off duty and wasn't supposed to be there anyway. By the way, I'm sorry to barge in on you at this hour."

"You didn't, I let you in." Helen smiled, weakly.

They sat in silence.

Cartwright plunged his face into his hands, breathing heavily.

"You ok?" She enquired.

"No, not really, but I better get going." Cartwright leaned forward preparing to stand.

"He's innocent, you know."

Cartwright stopped his movement and frowned, "Who?"

Helen held her stare.

Part 4 (Felix Baxter)

The Robot Man pulls his naked wife close to him and kisses the back of her neck, she groans with sleepy pleasure.

They lie, post-coital in the spoon position. His wife is

halfway to dreamland, but Felix Baxter is wide awake. The disposal of the analyst was just the final stepping stone in his game plan of making it to directorship level, nothing personal.

"That move had to have tipped me over the edge," he thought to himself. *"I've saved his company for god's sake. If that doesn't do it then nothing will!"*

Felix Baxter prides himself on being a man of quiet action. It is this quiet action that has earned him his current role of National Head of Robotics for one of the largest companies in the world. It is also the catalyst behind his spacious four bedroom Milton Keynes home, his gorgeous 27 year old wife and two beautiful little girls. And this self-same subtle but diligent action will be behind his promotion to International Head of Engineering, with its £300,000 a year salary.

The Robot Man smiles with satisfaction, then sleeps.

PART 25

"I can't talk to you about him, it's more than my job's worth." Tom Cartwright stood up and attempted to establish an air of authority.

"Look, I'm not sure what you guys think you know about Andrew Dax, but he's not a criminal, and frankly he's way too important to be detained as your scapegoat for the drone killings!"

Cartwright pointed at Helen sternly. "Hey! Be careful what you say to me, I'm still a policeman and..." he halted his sentence and frowned "Important? What do you mean, important?"

"I thought we weren't talking about him?" Helen taunted.

Cartwright cut his eyes and smirked subtly. "You're quite a piece of work, Ms Clyne."

"It's Helen, and look, you're off the clock right now aren't you?"

Cartwright nodded.

"Well can't we speak "off the record" just for a moment? No-one will know."

Cartwright sighed and retook his seat.

Helen leaned forward and lowered her voice. "I have a contact that knows Cleaver Corp inside out, he's a master hacker, a criminal, you would call him. Anyway, I strongly believe he could hold the key to the answers that we both seek."

14

A ndrew Dax lay on his back on his meagre bunker,
        hand on chest, listening intently to his heartbeat.
           Each soft "thud" was in stereo, due to the
enforced silence that encircled him.

The darkness was so dense that it seemed to press him
into the mattress. Although it could just as well have been
the downwards pressure of his predicament forcing his
head down into the thin pillow.

His gently knocking heart partially hypnotised him.

Ever since his "faux heart attack" episode, Dax had
been overly aware of that little fist sized muscle burrowed
within the centre-left of his chest.

The onsite physician would tell him that although
cardiac arrest and a severe anxiety attack can share several
common symptoms, there are subtle differences. For
instance, the chest pain from a heart attack is focused in
the centre of the chest and is crushing. It is usually persis-
tent, may radiate to the left arm, neck or back and lasts
longer than 5 - 10 minutes. Heart attack victims don't
hyperventilate, any tingling they experience is usually
confined to the left arm, and vomiting is common.

Conversely, during a panic attack, chest pain is localized over the heart and described as sharp, and comes and goes. The pain usually intensifies with breathing in and out. Panic attack may cause nausea, but vomiting is very rare. If tingling is present, the entire body tingles.

This news, along with the tests, which identified no immediate problems with the muscle or arteries, should have brought great comfort.

However, even the slightest irregularity in the pattern of each set of beats made him nervy, which in turn raised the overall pulse rate, which in turn made Dax suddenly not want to hear anymore.

Sometimes it seemed like the beating had slowed to a stop, sending him into a completely irrational frenzy. As if he could lie there and hear his heart stop and be able to react to this with any kind of action! This frenzy would threaten to bring on an attack, which in turn brought the elevated, pounding beats rushing back to the fore.

The beats slowed but became irregular again. The deeper recesses of his mind started to become sure that this cell would turn out to be his final resting place. The dread returned, Dax shot up from his bed (as if this would tear him from the jaws of ultimate mortality) and turned the pathetically dim light on. He stood, back against the wall and began his breathing exercises.

Believe it or not, this wasn't the ideal way to pass the time in there, at night, when sleep refused to come to the party

PART 26

The Power is shifting...

The Element moves, deliberately and balefully below us, and with each human life it feeds on, its self-awareness becomes stronger and more formidable.

It was roughly extracted from its home environment and forced into slavery in an environment that cannot sustain it efficiently. Whilst back then it was fearful and confused, it now knows that it is unfathomably stronger than the slave drivers that kidnapped it and have since mercilessly drawn on its essence. It is now calm, focussed, and intent on reversing the roles.

Due to its parthenogenetic nature it has multiplied substantially and now has its sights firmly set on mining its way to the core of this alien world. From there it can gain access to an almost unlimited source of human sustenance from every part of this weak, pathetic planet.

The Power is shifting...

The inferior organisms on this planet naively believed they could incarcerate it within a small metallic prison.

Now it is intent on revenge. It will start slowly, with fear. Each time it multiplies it sends shockwaves through this world which reverberate through to the surface and interferes with the senses of its colonies. It's pleased with the panic that this generates. At present, it only feeds when needed, but before long it will eat aggressively.

The goal: extermination. Eventually, this feeble planet will become home, fully and completely, and will be stronger for it.

The Power is shifting.

PART 27

Tom Cartwright sat, hunched forward on the one-seater in the corner of Helen's living room, staring at the Portentis Engine printouts, wide eyed and motionless.

The journalist had just given him the unabridged version of the situation with The Bear and Andrew Dax. At first the young officer had refused to believe that this person could know so much about the inner workings and covert future plans of Cleaver Corp. At one point he even threatened to arrest her on the grounds of attempting to pervert the course of justice and conspiring with a felon.

It wasn't until she had shown him the crumpled readings and explained that getting them decoded was the one and only way that either of them had any chance of finding the truth behind their siblings' untimely demise.

The only person who had the ability to achieve this was the faceless, ghost-like hacker.

"I've never even heard of this Bear character, he isn't on any radar at Enforcements, I would know." Cartwright spoke but didn't look up from the paper.

"He says that's why he's managed to glean so much, because he's not motivated by money, power or notoriety. He denies the perception that he's a fraudster or thief, classing himself as a whistle blower who craves truth."

Cartwright dropped the printouts onto his lap, leant back and exhaled heavily.

Helen stared at the young officer. She knew that her only hope of getting to Dax was through this man.

"Do you actually know Andrew Dax?" she asked.

"We've met at work in passing." Cartwright remained in his position and spoke to the ceiling.

"He seemed like a decent enough bloke." He finally lowered his head to meet Helen's eye line.

"I actually did his incarceration interview and paperwork after he was picked up."

Cartwright grimaced in acknowledgement of his error. He had already disclosed way too much.

Cartwright figured the damage had already been done, and so decided to finally explain the situation with Andrew Dax at Central Enforcements in its entirety.

Helen Clyne went on to challenge the young officer on why or even how Dax, a data analyst from a completely different division would feel the need to tamper with the programme settings of high tech machinery that he had absolutely no experience with.

Admittedly, some of the most notoriously devious crimes in history had been committed by the most unassuming antagonists.

What would be the motivation that would make a straight laced, long serving techy decide to deviate from his day to day role to such an extent? Could all this be in the name of mischief or anarchy?

The fact that Dax had been charged with manslaughter and not murder meant that Cleaver Corp themselves had submitted to the fact that causing death wasn't the end game.

Even Cartwright admitted that something didn't sit right with the way the analyst had been treated thus far.

The conversation swung back and forth.

Helen remained cross-legged on the floor, but Cartwright stood up and paced. "Ok, let's say he is innocent. Let's say that somehow a meeting between Dax and this Bear character was achieved. I want answers as much as you do, but there would need to be a bigger agenda. Finding out Portentis is dangerous is one thing, but Cleaver Corp are big enough to coast through that kind of problem. For me to put my job and possibly my freedom on the line by even considering breaking this man out there would have to be more, a lot more!"

"More?" Helen said, eyebrows raised, "Oh ok, you need more convincing!" She sprung up from her carpeted seat and rummaged in the drawer of a sideboard on the adjacent corner of the living room, but said nothing.

Cartwright looked on expectantly. She pulled out a small, black device.

Three days ago, The Bear had sent Helen a package, the following day she received this message:-

If the Analyst is being held at Central Enforcements, like you guess he is, he won't be held there indefinitely. The facilities there are not equipped for long term holding. Sooner or later he will be moved. When that happens, I'm positive that it will be a Commissar that will transport him. This is all conjecture mind you, however if the situation is as you believe it is, this will work. However you will need someone on

the inside, but I have no doubt in your ability to achieve this.

The package I've sent to you contains a device that comprises of two separate parts. Operation is very simple:-

The larger, oval shaped device needs to be plugged into the USB port in the underside of the operational dashboard of the Commissar training pod – Note, it is imperative that the training pod is used and no other. This needs to be done 15 minutes before the Commissar leaves with Dax (it doesn't matter which unit is used or what direction they are going in, as long as that particular pod is linked to the Commissar unit).

The smaller, square shaped device just needs to be hidden anywhere on the Analyst's person.

The device within the pod needs to be plugged in and unhampered for a full 10 minutes from when they depart.

That's it, nothing more, nothing less, I will do everything else. As soon as the screen in the pod goes blank, whoever you get to do this just needs to take out the device and leave the pod, raising the fact that the station has shut down mid operation. They can even destroy the receiver once the 10 minutes is up.

I can make the whole thing look like a malfunction.

Tom Cartwright sat, frozen to the spot, in a state of disbelief "My god, he knows everything, to the absolute, bloody letter!"

And with that the young officer was sold.

Helen held the two parts of the device in each hand as she took a seat on the three-seater opposite the young officer. "I have no idea how he knows what he knows, but I think we need to count it as a positive that he's on our side, even if it is only to an extent."

"Ok, so what now?" Cartwright asked quietly.

Helen grimaced as the gravity of what she was asking of this relative stranger started to hit home. She stared at Cartwright guiltily.

Realisation marked Cartwright's face.

"You expect me to do it? Oh I don't know about this!" Cartwright looked down, shaking his head gravely.

"All you would have to do is give the small device to Dax, then plug the other one in. That's all. Dax would simply disappear after that."

Cartwright rolled his eyes "Oh yeah simple, and what happens when he doesn't arrive at Belmarsh? You think they'll just go "oops we've lost one, oh well he wasn't too dangerous!" No, they'll catch him, come directly to me as the chief investigator, and then I'm screwed!"

Helen frowned. "Does the Bear seem to you like a person that leaves things to chance? For 15 years this guy's been a complete ghost! Believe me, if he hides Dax he will NOT be found, I don't care how good Cleaver Corp think they are!"

Cartwright breathed deeply and rubbed his temples. "Shit, shit, shit!" He began to tremble again, the experiences of the last few days, again began to take their toll.

"I... I just want a good future for the next generation, you know? At first it seemed like the Corp had all the answers, I was actually happy there. But now, my god! It's not just what's happening with Portentis, it's these Commissars! I mean what the hell is that all about! No one seems to be batting an eyelid! I'm hearing rumours of weirder and weirder stuff going on in shady research labs, and not just at Sanhedrin either." He sighed and took another deep breath "But why me, why is it my arse on the line? No, it's just too big! Surely someone else should be doing something?"

His voice wobbled with emotion. "I… I just wanted to be a copper, you know?"

Helen went over and crouched before the young officer and put her hand on his. He looked up and met her eye line, his eyes glistening with tears.

"This is the only hope for change," Helen said softly, "the Bear sees Dax as the last piece in the puzzle, and you've already said you have your doubts whether Dax is even guilty! Just go talk to him, you know, question him and see what you think. If we could get them together… all the dark secrets? All the lies? A real explanation as to how we lost our relatives? All out in the open."

Tears ran down Cartwright's face. Helen squeezed his hand tightly and continued.

"This is the only way."

PART 28

Cartwright sat staring at the two part device resting on the coffee table in the middle of his living room.

He picked up the Bear's instructions and read them again. The process the hacker had laid out was simple enough and by all accounts would be over in minutes, but what then? The young officer's mind swung back and forth. How could he trust the word of a criminal and put everything he had strived for on the line for a person he hardly knew?

The evidence against Andrew Dax seemed extremely conclusive, so why couldn't he shake the feeling that some form of foul play had been involved with the convenient and neat way in which his former colleague had been arrested and jailed?

The Met Police had already been a privatised company for several years when Cartwright was recruited, and at that time he didn't share the suspicion that a lot of his peers directed at the organisation that paid his wages.

However, in Cartwright's mind, the evidence had been stacking up against Cleaver Corp for the last two years.

The young officer was trying to balance out the bitterness he felt at the slow and steady marginalisation of his role, with his genuine mistrust of the organisation. If the latter turned out to be the heavier, then doing this could be the only way to generate change.

There was nothing else for it, he needed a showdown with the analyst.

PART 29

Andrew Dax slumped back in his plastic moulded seat.

His skin was pallid from lack of sunlight and his body was starting to show signs of malnutrition. Being sat in a small room without windows for three weeks, only eating half portions of a lukewarm meal each day begins to tell on the body a lot sooner than one might think.

"Ah Consultation Room 1, it's become like an old friend to me," Dax croaked with sarcastic nostalgia.

As the Chief Investigator in the drone/Manslaughter case, Tom Cartwright was able to arrange a short notice meeting with Dax under the façade of "further questioning."

He had lead the bedraggled and weak analyst through to the closest consultation room, where he secretly switched off the surveillance monitor.

Cartwright sat, fist on chin, staring at Dax thoughtfully. Silence.

"What?" Dax barked, shrugging in frustration.

"You've lost weight," Cartwright motioned finally, flicking a point in the analyst's direction.

"Oh thanks coach, finally some acknowledgement for signing up to the *Get banged Up, Then get the same Horrible, Cold, Inedible Shit thrown at you 4 Days out of a Week* diet."

Cartwright smiled sympathetically.

"Is there a reason why you've brought me here?" Dax asked gruffly.

Cartwright said nothing, visibly choosing his words. He finally leaned forward. "How's it going in here, have you and your lawyer made much progress?"

"What do you care?"Dax frowned.

"Well the more progress you can make here, before you're moved, the better." Cartwright drummed his fingertips on the cold steel work top.

"Hmm well, as I'm sure you already know, I'm being moved in two days. So times kind of up, progress-wise."

Cartwright persevered with apparent genuine concern. "We've not had anyone in holding for this long before. How are you being treated down here?"

Dax stared at the Officer and pursed his lips.

Finally he sighed deeply "Look, Cleaver Corp needed a scapegoat for the drone killings, I get it. But…"

He squeezed his eyes shut, trying to repress his emotions. "…but this isolation shit, man this just feels snide, you know? It might sound pathetic, but I… I just want to speak to my folks, what harm could that do?!"

Tears trickled down his cheeks and he buried his face in his hands, unable to hold down his sorrow any longer.

"Why are they doing this to me? Who am I? I'm nobody, just a data-geek. Surely they could have found a more fitting patsy, you know, like someone who actually knows how to use the bloody things?"

Dax sobbed unashamedly.

Cartwright felt a warm wave of pity for the analyst

wash over him, the hunch he had upon first meeting him was now confirmed. He was now certain of this man's innocence.

He stood and rubbed Dax's shoulder. "Ok look, if you didn't do it, then have you any idea who might have?" he asked quietly.

Dax cleared his throat and sniffed loudly, attempting to compose himself, "I have my suspicions, but you wouldn't believe me," he crocked.

Cartwright used the hand that rested on the analyst's shoulder and turned him so they were eye to eye. "Try me."

"What is this? What's going on? If this is a trap…"

"It's not" Cartwright cut in, retaking his seat.

He took a tiny, black, oval shaped object from his inside pocket and held it out, staring at the analyst.

Dax looked at the device then looked up at Cartwright blankly.

"You tell me who you think it was, and I'll tell you what this is, and believe me, *you* want to know what this is."

15

PART 1 (WEDNESDAY 28TH NOVEMBER - THE DAY
BEFORE ANDREW DAX IS MOVED)

E zekiel Cleaver speaks with the Prime Minister over the phone:-

PM: "That's excellent news! When will you be ready to make your statement?"

Cleaver: "I think it might be best to hold off until the analyst is off site and secured at Belmarsh."

PM: "Yes I tend to agree, and the PI Immunity order will allow us to keep his identity and location classified long term?"

Cleaver: "Yes Sir, it will remain sealed shut."

PM: "Good, good. Begin preparing the press statement now; there shouldn't be too much time between the move and the statement. The sooner we can get the public back on board, the sooner the drones can be put back to work.

I just want to take this opportunity to commend you and your team on the prompt and efficient way that you have managed to resolve this potentially catastrophic issue. You've once again shown that you're still the man for the job!"

Cleaver: "Thank you Sir, you're too gracious!"

Part 2 (Wednesday 28th November)

Dax sat on his bunk, staring at the tiny 1cm by 1cm, black square device.

Tomorrow this tiny object would become the rather uncomfortable filling in a "clenched butt cheek sandwich," lovingly prepared by the analyst himself. Tom Cartwright had insisted on this most violating of hiding places, as this "pocket" was most likely to mask the device from the complex's many surveillance and scanning systems.

Andrew Dax, at first treated this sudden olive branch with the cynicism he thought it deserved, "Oh yeah, you're gonna bust me out of the pen! Sure, right!"

It wasn't until the officer admitted that his sister had met a similar end to the one that befell Robert Clyne. This along with the gruesome recount of the "burning boy," had made Dax a little more receptive.

Besides, it wasn't as if he was a member of the decision making committee anyway. The only choices that lay under the analyst's jurisdiction were: an increasingly likely, long stretch in Belmarsh's "Big Boy" Prison or a life in hiding, working alongside Europe's most notorious and mysterious hacker, forming a kind of underground myth-busters duo!

Again he started to feel like a pawn. However at least victory for these particular players would result in Dax avoiding prison, and who knows maybe someday even a pardon.

"The whole thing should be done in 25 minutes, with very minimal input by us. Just shove it up there, get in the back of the van and say nothing, the Bear will do the rest." Cartwright seemed to really believe in this shadowy figure.

This surprised Dax somewhat, and he sensed that a feeling of betrayal and desperation fuelled the young offi-cer's actions.

Between 8:30am and 9:30am tomorrow would now be the most pivotal moment in Andrew Dax's life. The result of that one single hour would literally determine the direction of the rest of the analyst's life.

"Well, I'd better eat all my dinner tonight!" he sighed.

Part 3 (Wednesday 28th November)

"The training pod? Why the hell are you using that thing?" Robson asked roughly.

Cartwright stood in the Chief's office, heart racing. He had just informed his boss of his intention to use the training pod tomorrow to control Jason Sark in the transportation of Andrew Dax.

"Well, to be honest Sir, it's kind of my maiden voyage with a Commissar, and I really just wanted to be as comfortable as possible. You know, just until I build up some confidence."

"Confidence?" Robson smiled, "You ain't never had any problem with that, Tommy."

Cartwright chuckled plastically, "Yeah well, ever since you mentioned your faith in me in taking the step up to Detective, I've wanted to tighten up my game from all angles."

The young officer felt equally impressed and concerned by the ease in which the convincing cover story came to him.

"Ok, son," Robson said quietly, his face softened, "and you're sure you're up to it? Coz if you ain't?"

"No Sir, I want to do it. I'm just trying to get back to normal, you know?"

Part 4 (Thursday 29th November – The day of the Move)

The time is 2:45am and Helen Clyne is awake.

She had dozed off a couple of hours ago, only to be jolted awake by a nightmare which involved Robbie inter-spliced with the Cartwright's burning boy. The Bear had seemingly covered all the bases, but there was still so much that could go wrong.

What if, upon grilling Dax, Tom Cartwright wasn't convinced and decided it wasn't worth the risk?

What if they decide to have a trainee shadow the officer whilst he operates the commissar?

Oh god, what if Dax himself decides that he is in enough trouble as it is and refuses to comply?

The horrible helplessness returned.

16

The time was 8:17am and Tom Cartwright was feeling nauseous, having just plugged the receiver device into the USB port in the training pod.

"No one ever goes in there, no one ever goes in there," he chanted to himself.

He walked briskly across the Central Enforcements main office and down the stairs towards the holding wing, stills of every scenario in which the next hour could wrong flashed through his mind.

"Morning Officer." The guard said, his tone, annoyingly chirpy.

"Morning mate, just come to pick up the analyst." Cartwright did his best to *out-chirp* the guard.

"Yeah, I know. The big lad's already down there," the guard said as he pressed the sensor and let Cartwright across the threshold.

As he walked down the dim corridor, Cartwright saw Sark's huge silhouette stood still, guard-like outside Dax's cell. As he approached, Jason Sark spun to face him. Cartwright held up his ID.

After a couple of seconds the machines focussing

227

mechanism kicked in, the soft whirring sound emitting from behind its eyes made the officer's blood run cold. Sark turned and opened the thick cell door.

Cartwright didn't actually need to be down there, he could just as well have begun controlling the massive Commissar from the pod. However he decided to take this gamble, as he was overcome by the need to look Dax in the eye one more time, just to ensure it was still on.

The look Dax gave the officer as he snapped the handcuffs across his wrists, told him that, for better or worse, this thing was definitely about to happen.

Cartwright waited just long enough to see Dax disappear around the corner led by the machine, before making a bee-line back upstairs. He had to check his pace several times as his nerves kept speeding him up.

Part 2 (Thursday 29th November - The day of the Move)

The training pod had never felt so small.

Cartwright felt tight-chested and claustrophobic. However at least the device was still plugged in and didn't seem to have been disrupted. He looked at his watch. 8:30 exactly. "Right 10 minutes, nearly there!"

He set the stop clock on the time piece.

The commissar and its cargo were already on the road. The units were so advanced that once moving, they pretty much controlled themselves, leaving the controller with a simple monitoring responsibility. Although right now Cartwright would have preferred something more to do than watch the road go by. He checked the stop clock... 6 minutes.

Voices hummed uncomfortably close to the curtain that he sat behind.

"Cartwright," the voice emerged just above the busy humming outside.

The officer froze, listening intently, hoping the call was his imagination messing with him. "Cartwright!"

This time almost a shout, it was Robson. "Shit!"

Cartwright hissed, crouching forward. He looked at the stop clock... 4 minutes.

The screen was still on and capturing the vehicle in motion. He recognised the fleet-footed approaching foot-steps. Cartwright looked around helplessly. "Cartwright," Robson called again. "This can't be happening!" he thought, beads of chilly sweat sprung from every pore. The curtain wobbled, announcing the Chief's arrival.

If Robson decided to pull the curtain back, it was all over!

"Sir?" Cartwright finally answered his voice quiet and shaky. "How's it going in there, pal?"

The curtain wobbled again.

No, no... please!

"Erm, yeah not bad, nearly done," Cartwright adjusted his sitting position, attempting to hide the device. His boss' silhouette hung on the other side of the curtain.

"Not letting that famous lack of confidence get to you then?" the Chief chuckled playfully.

2 minutes...

"Ha, nah course not, you know me!" A ray of hope shone on the officer, as he realised his voice sounded quite convincing.

"Ha! Good, good!" The curtain wobbled again, but this time in reaction to his boss walking away. Cartwright collapsed backwards in his seat and exhaled heavily, his heart still hammered against his ribcage as if trying to escape. He looked at the screen as street after street rolled by as if nothing had happened, the mute Commissar navi-gating each turn with sterile precision.

He ducked his head to check on the receiver, it remained in place. The volume of the voices outside rose.

He looked at the stop clock... 4.3.2.1...

The dashboard remained on, but the vehicle on screen came to a screeching halt.

Angry horns blared.

Cartwright held his breath...

Then a soft electrical whirring sound... a frantic mess of data suddenly replaced the street picture...the whirring became louder.

Cartwright looked around helplessly. "What the hell's happening?"

Then the screen turned black.

17

ANDREW DAX

I'm walking at a furious pace, breathing in short sharp bursts between my teeth.

Must get to Welwyn station for the meet. Better check my pace actually, it's going to be very long walk!

Unfortunately being an escaped fugitive is not really conducive to a smooth exit from any given major city, it also doesn't lend itself to the luxuries of public transport.

Why the hell did I sell my car again?

Oh well no matter, I have legs, and besides everything that I need is either snugly nestled between my cheeks, or safely stored in my memory banks.

Besides, driving wouldn't have been an option anyway.

It's now way too risky for me to physically write any musings or events from here on in.

In light of this, you are hesitantly invited into my internal dialogue...

Welcome, please tread lightly.

I look back over my shoulder, just in time to see the black private ambulance disappear over the horizon, navigated by puppet number two.

I feel a swell of gratitude, but can't help but feel a tail-sting of remorse for the amount that Tom and Helen lay on the line to see me free.

You see when I tampered with those commands last year, I didn't intend for Units 8 and 14 to actually cause that level of harm. I was indeed set up, but maybe not in the way that you may have been thinking. I'm a very careful person, and I know for a fact that I covered my tracks adequately, after doing what I did. This means whoever uncovered my actions knew exactly how and where to look. Not only that, but they had the ability to make it very easy for the next passer-by to stumble upon my ill-fated plot. I believe the only thing that would have surprised my pursuer was the fact that I myself was that passer-by.

Now please believe me, the awareness that I am, in reality guilty of Manslaughter via Autonomous by Proxy does eat me up.

However, if you were to ask me if there was a means of going back in time, would I undo what I did, the answer would be an unyielding no. I acted out of necessity.

Now bear with me.

I'm no sociopath; I would like to think quite the opposite.

What you need to realise is I know something.

Something that some (maybe even your good self) had been harbouring concerns about all along.

What I know is directly connected to Ezekiel Cleaver and he knows what I know.

In my eyes, Cleaver is an irresponsible liar. Whether he is genuinely evil or not, remains to be seen.

Confused?

Ok let me ask you this, what do the majority of living organisms have in common?

- They eat

- They grow

So why should this fail to be the case for Niroplaxia Gamonite?

At this point I feel it only right to apologise, you see although I haven't lied directly, I haven't been entirely straight with you either. You see whilst the panic attacks I had been suffering from were very real, the so called self-blogging therapy although brushed upon by a counsellor, was in fact the start of a memoir to be found in case of a situation of this exact nature. I had to be very careful when writing it however. It had to inform, but on the other hand could not incriminate me.

Let me start from the top.

I've been working for Cleaver Corp for over 5 years; making my way up to lead data analyst in the chain between the Portentis Engine and the Computer Room, and everything in between. This affords a few perks, such as a very reasonable salary for my age. Along with pension and health benefits, my own broom cupboard/office, and finally, and most relevantly, an access (almost) all areas pass to the Sanhedrin.

Some months back when I said I was receiving strange readings from the engine, well it wasn't the first time.

Two years ago, whilst at my work station, I starting picking up some aggressively irregular coding inflections via my engine port way. For some reason (probably, because I was newly promoted and had just received my shiny new backstage pass) I told no one and decided to go down to the mole's lair and investigate the source of the readings myself.

I took the lift down as far as it would take me, the lifts within the complex end two floors before sub cellar, not sure why. A strange sensation overwhelmed me upon starting the steps, a deep throbbing that I felt more than heard, a feeling so intense that I had to hold on to the railings to steady myself, the pressure in my inner ears was unbearable. I thought I'd gone deaf until shouting voices became apparent from within sub cellar; something was going seriously wrong in there!

As I approached the thick steel automatic doors, the unsettling sensation began to ease. I didn't expect my pass to take me any further (and it hasn't since) but I lifted it to the scan panel and the doors slid open.

To explain exactly what I saw in detail would be futile, as you wouldn't believe me, but to summarize, I witnessed panic, confusion and fear. From that very moment it became glaringly apparent that it was only a matter of time before the Portentis Engine would no longer be able to contain the angry, growing LC Element living within it. Technicians were frantically working away, attempting to batten down any and every weakness that presented itself along the surface bodywork of the capsule.

Despite their efforts, the organism seemed to writhe randomly in every which direction under the tough outer shell of the engine. My eyes were drawn to the pulsing glow coming from underneath it. The moles were understandably preoccupied with their desperate attempts to prevent the life form from escaping; leaving the building and the surrounding area vulnerable to god knows what fate! I stood staring, momentarily transfixed by the glow. I was, at that moment, absolutely certain that this thing was attempting to burrow its way under the streets of the City

"Oi, you, out!" The shout shook me out of my daze. I looked down. A particularly small mole stood right before me, well under my eye line, scowling. I didn't get chance to respond before he shoved me backwards as the steel door simultaneously slid shut.

If I'd have had the balls I would have blown the whistle

immediately, but since the mole that kicked me out and I became locked in a metaphorical game of chicken in the week that followed, as to who was going to escalate the issue to management first, I took the cowards way out and said nothing. Maybe it was the desire to protect my job, or maybe I was simply kidding myself into believing that the moles had sorted out whatever problem had occurred down there. However when you attempt to bury the memory of seeing something that disturbing and potentially destructive, even when you think it's gone, it simply lies dormant for a time. When it did decide to start re-emerging it was violent and tumorous, manifesting itself in anxiety attacks.

The episodes grew in severity, until finally I decided to act.

So the plan went something like this...

I don't like CLEDs, I believe that has been well established. So I decided, rather audaciously, to kill two proverbial birds with one stone. I did a little boning up on CLED commands and programming (when you train as a Data Analyst it is inevitable that you will pick up some basic programming principles along the way). With this knowledge gained, I went about the covert task of using a couple of the drones to destroy two of Portentis Power's roadside transformer boxes, thus achieving public doubt in the machines' capabilities along with thrusting the spotlight squarely onto Portentis Power.

There would surely have to be full investigations into both companies after an incident of that severity.

Now I didn't take on a massively risky challenge like this in a frivolous manner, it actually took a year of meticulous planning and research into CLEDs and the history behind not only the discovery of the LC Element, but also Cleaver Corp in general (you might have found my in-depth knowledge around Cleaver Corp and the Element a little odd, given my self-professed boredom with the place, well now you know).

The first unit was set to riddle one of transformer boxes with bullets, in broad daylight. The other was programmed to crush the hell out of the second box, I timed the latter to take place in the small hours of the morning.

I admit the plan backfired spectacularly! And please believe me, the guilt ties me in knots. In my earlier entries, the disconnected, even mildly flippant tone used when referring to the incidents, was pure ruse. Words can't express the despair I felt as I stood and took in the bold printed headline before me on that grey Monday morning. I had a decision to make, did I turn myself in and face jail, even though my intentions were one hundred percent honourable? Did I take myself out of the equation, knowing what I know?

Or did I say nothing, bide my time and come up with a new plan? After all there was still a chance that those people didn't die in vain. Now depending on whether you are a glass half full or glass half empty person would mould how you viewed the fact that the decision was abruptly taken out my hands by whoever uncovered my well buried tracks.

The death of Robert Clyne absolutely confirmed the malignant nature of the growing LC Element. It also confirmed that it is indeed highly dangerous. It absolutely was Niroplaxia Gamonite that killed him, and that horrendous incident could just be the tip of the iceberg! I know Cleaver knows this, and if he refuses to do anything about it, I reluctantly take on the responsibility of spreading this devastating gospel to all that will listen. Can its growth be stopped, or at least stemmed? I have no idea, but I have to try.

So that's why I have "Drive 16" securely stored in my

brain. You see Drive 16 is a set of codes that I have been memorising ever since the drone incident. The codes that make up drive 16, not only hold important stuff about Portentis Power's surge problem but when unencrypted it contains lots of other juicy data that I believe the Bear will be salivating at the prospect of getting his hands on. Put that with whatever it is I have up my arse, and you have quite a tool for change!

The Bear and I can then get to the task of identifying exactly what is going on beneath these City streets, in a view to blowing the lid off this whole mess. If (and this is a massive if!) we succeed in laying the foundations of Portentis Power's demise, I will gladly turn myself in and accept my punishment for the three fatalities. I would then at least be safe in the knowledge that I have had a hand in saving dozens, possibly hundreds more from the fate that befell Robert Clyne and Kim Cartwright. Nonetheless, for now I am the only conduit to the truth. Will another eventually build the courage to come forward and fly in the face of the juggernaut that is Cleaver Corp? Maybe, but there simply isn't time to wait for that. I'm getting way ahead of myself. None of these grand plans will come to fruition unless I actually get to the Bear in one piece without getting caught. So, I'd better get a move on.

My name is Andrew and I've been told that I think too deeply about things.

ACKNOWLEDGMENTS

ABOUT THE AUTHOR

D.R Linton's writing CV originally consisted solely of songs and screenplays. Khaos Engine is his debut Novella and is the first story in the *Khaos Engine* Trilogy. D.R Linton's fascination with human actions and reactions, drive most of his artistic endeavours.

He resides in the West Midlands UK, with his wife and son.

Printed in Great Britain
by Amazon